OF SINS & PSYCHOS

AK KOONCE

OF SINS AND PSYCHOS

A.K. KOONCE

To Sophie!

AKoonce

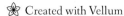

FOREWORD

Please be advised *Of Sins and Psychos* has reference to physical rape, and mind rape that could be triggering to some readers.

This is the glittering, drunken vomit of a tale of Bellatrix Cuore. It's a beautiful mess of inky words and tainted memories I'll never be able to forget. In summary, it's the tragedy that started my life.

And ruined hers.

She's the very heart of this story. And I guess that would just make the Carnal Brothers the blood and guts strung out in between . . .

PROLOGUE
TWENTY-FOUR YEARS EARLIER

SHE WAS BORN with a heart defect . . . several of them, Dr. Holland said.

The statistics that streamed all around us for the next twelve hours after our baby girl's birth were more than my mind could handle. Grief and fear are blinding emotions. They tend to block a lot of life out entirely.

But I remember some of them. *Seventy-five days.* That's how long it would take to get my baby a transplant. Her tiny heart had to hold on for seventy-five days. And along the way, her kidneys could shut down. Have you ever considered what a premature baby on dialysis might look like? Because the moment Dr. Holland said it, I thought it. And it's all I've thought about all night.

"Get some sleep, Brenda," Collin whispers to me from the other side of the hospital room. The faint sound of beeping monitors and nurses walking the halls just outside our small room are suddenly heard when I look up at him.

His emerald eyes are like hers. Except his are ringed with dark circles tonight.

We wondered for months what she would look like. Whose features our beautiful baby would take in. We never thought for a second one of us might have a tragic genetic trait to gift to her. A weak heart. She inherited that from my side, apparently.

"I'm just going to go check on her one more time." I stand, and my entire body feels battered and worn. A tremor shakes through my frame from the weight my legs don't want to hold.

Collin doesn't respond. He stares, lost in the dark nothingness of the room as I slip by his chair.

The socks the hospital gave me scuff along the glossy white tile. At my side, my IV drip skirts around with a bad wheel twirling without care.

"Should get some rest, Mrs. Cuore." The nurse behind the counter gives me a tense smile, but I know she won't stop me.

New mothers are made entirely of worry. I expected to check on my sweet baby for cries, or shallow breathing, or wet diapers.

I didn't expect this.

Down to the neonatal intensive care unit I shuffle. It's farther away than the nursery. I still have to pass by the glass window of healthy babies sleeping soundly.

I don't look at them.

A nurse with a clipboard is at the desk across from the NICU. Her brown eyes shine with a soft, knowing smile when she looks at me.

I wash my hands as she gathers up a blue gown in silence. It's a strange, stilted process. Like my baby is on loan, and I'm just a recurring customer.

She ties the back of my sterile gown and opens the door for me. It slides closed without a sound, and she watches me for a moment through the glass of the door. I feel her watching me. I feel all of them watching me.

Waiting for me to break.

There's only one carriage now. The other that was here this morning is gone. I now have privacy with my baby girl, and that only makes my emotions rise up with pain.

"Bellatrix," I coo to her, my voice breaking against her name as I bend down low with tears dampening my lashes.

They try to make it feel normal. A frilly, pink cloth covers the hard metal of the cart they call a bassinet. It's a nice touch, but it's still just hiding the truth: my baby won't make it seventy-five days. If by some miracle she does, a transplant heart only has a fifteen to twenty-five year life expectancy.

And then what?

Golden light shines down on her, warming her and providing the body heat her heart is too weak to give. At over two months early, her body is frail, skinny for an infant who should have lovely rolls and plump

3

cheeks. The graying tone of her skin makes me want to pick her up and hold her close to my chest, apologize for giving her the worst feature I didn't even know I possessed.

A weak heart.

Tears stream down my face as helplessness finally sinks into me. The nurse outside the door is turned to her desk, oblivious to me as I sink to my knees and pray. My hands hover over her little body, not wanting to disturb the tubes and wires haloing around her. All the years I went to Catholic school don't seem sufficient for such a request. I need more than a prayer. I need more than help. I need . . .

"Please help her," I sob into the pink, frilly cloth. "P —Please—"

I don't know why I did it. I'll never tell Collin. I'll never tell anyone.

Because when a calm, dark voice beneath that bassinet asked to save my baby, I gave her to him.

CHAPTER ONE

Bella

The wind catches my dark locks while I stand on a single wobbling leg. In one clutched hand, I have my phone and purse . . . in the other: a possible disaster waiting to happen. My keys and Starbucks are in danger as I also grip an enormous glittering, pink box. The white bow atop blows in the cool night air. My right knee is trying to hoist the gift higher but failing miserably. I lean into the trunk of my old Pontiac Grand Am like it's a dirty one night stand I'll never remember.

This single disastrous moment feels like a summary of my entire year. Hell, maybe my entire life.

Then with a slow, focused breath, everything calms.

I've got it. I got it. It's fine. I won't drop my little sister's *ridiculously* heavy gift of books I snagged in the best bookstores in Chicago. I'm still the cool older sister who may or may not have ended her year-and-a-half relationship with her shitty ex-boyfriend, dropped out of U of C, and started secretly pole dancing to cover rent. Not that Ivy knows that. So yeah, I'm every thirteen-year-old girl's aspiration in life.

I. Fucking. Got. This.

With the corner of my thumb, I click the little lock button on my key fob.

Except . . .

The panic alarm blares.

A flickering, golden light illuminates my parent's blissfully quiet suburbia. The neighbor, Mrs. Donnelly, flips on her entry light like her hand has been on the switch since I pulled in.

"*Shit. Shit. Shit.*" The coffee is the first to make its escape from being seen with me. It goes down in a splatter of cold, caramelly frappe all over my leggings.

"Mother-fucking-over-priced-coffee-bean-addiction!"

The shiny box teeters against my hand and knee once more. On a fumbling lack of stability, I grind into the back of my Grand Am like it's Pete Davidson's notorious monster coc—

"Bella? Bella is that you? Why are you making so much noise? It's ten o'clock at night, hunny."

My phone and purse drop from my other hand. Partly because I'm a mess and partly because I'm a problem solver. Now that I can finally get an actual grip on the box of bargain books, I give my mom a tense smile. Then rather unattractively, I blow my hair from my face. A look of poise filters into place. My thumb clicks over the key fob, and silence falls. I slam the trunk closed and ignore the purse, phone, and spilled coffee—only kicking the little plastic cup slightly on my way to the front door.

"Mom!" I beam a smile. A real one. One I haven't felt in a long, long time.

My boots squeak when I reach the red front door, and my mother's blue eyes are filled with concern when she looks at me. Just like she has for the last eight years. Ever since I came back . . . Ever since he took me . . .

"Your purse, dear." She pulls her white robe closed and I try to stop her when she rushes past me to grab my abandoned belongings in the driveway.

I'd be worried, too, but this isn't Chicago. Nashville, Illinois is the polar opposite of my day-to-day city life. I'd be more likely to get attacked by a rogue deer than I am to get my purse stolen on a Saturday night in the midwestern suburbs. The handbag would still be there when dawn cracked over its spilled contents and the newly shattered glass that's surely slashed down the front of my cell phone.

"What are you doing here?" she asks as she shuts the door softly behind her. Her small frame is just like Ivy's. Ivy got the good genes. The petite, blonde hair, blue-eyed genes. While I took after my father. A fucking six-foot-five Viking of a man. "Why didn't you call? Is something wrong? Did Jonathon . . . did he have another outburst? You know that's not good for your heart, hunny."

Her attention flits to the strawberry birthmark that splatters across my chest, but I ignore her worry as I have since the day I was born.

And yes. Jonathon did have another *outburst*. Several over the last few months. The final one left both of my arms bruised and my lip swollen for weeks.

That was the last of Jonathon. Not because we had a bad breakup, but because men . . . they have to be careful when mistreating a woman who has friends like I do.

"I ended things." Perfect phrasing. Ended. Things were definitely gruesomely ended for Jonathon.

I understand what abuse is. I saw him for what he was. I'm just an optimist. People like me always think things will get better. That it wasn't that bad. We trudge on toward that golden horizon of a future.

Until we fucking snap.

"Aww, Bella Hunny. I'm so glad you're here, no matter what the circumstances." She pulls me in against her chest, the birthday box poking hard into my ribs as I shift around it to hug her.

"God, Mom. No. Gross. I'm not here because of him." I blow my hair from my face once more, pulling back to show her my prize possession. Thirteen books.

Each individually wrapped in magazine and newspaper clippings, whatever had the best aesthetically written words scribed over the pages to convey the surprise hidden book inside. I ripped apart multiple arrest sections to cover the crime and thriller books. I even shredded apart many bridal magazines for the romcom novels, which was in fact really good for my mental health, because let's face it, I'd rather join a radical, crazed cult than enter into a legal, binding contract of marriage to any man. *Ever*. Let those bridal pages rip!

The inside of this sparkly, pink box really shows how much I want my baby sister to enjoy the pages she gets lost in when she reads.

Yeah. I'm fucking proud of my gift. It's fucking amazing, if I do say so myself.

I shake the box enticingly at my mom, my smile growing by the second.

"Is she still up?"

"Who?" Mom asks, but I'm too excited to fully hear her.

"It's only ten. Iv! Ivy get your ass up!" I yell up the stairs, my anticipation bubbling to see my sister after months of just texts and quick video chats.

"Shhh! Your father's watching the news in bed," she hisses.

I can't quite explain it. During my bouncing excitement, the chill of the cold frappe seeping through my leggings, and the deep line that creases my mother's brow, realization tries tapping against my stubborn skull.

But I ignore it.

Just like I did the night I came home. And no one noticed I'd been missing for nearly a year. At sixteen I'd vanished from their lives, but they . . . hadn't noticed.

That scar on my cheek? Just ignore it? The night terrors that haunted me every. Single. Night? Just ignore it. The special diet of sleeping pills Mom and my therapist both agreed on . . .

Ignore it. That's what my family is good at.

I guess it's still what I'm doing. Right now.

"Bella!" My dad's cheery smile is oblivious to my twisting emotions and my mother's panicked concern.

He always is. Sometimes to be oblivious is the only way to keep a hold of that faltering happiness in our lives.

But he never treated me like I was fragile. Not like my mother does. Years of missed sports and sitting on the bleachers have made me bitter at my own fragile heart.

Which might be why I started dancing.

"Where the hell is Iv! Is she at her friend's house tonight? I know I'm late. She knew I was coming though. We had plans. We were going to watch SNL and TikToks until the sun came up." Because, ya know, Pete Davidson.

My stream of words only causes that etching line to seep deeper between her pale brows. I know that look of confused worry. It's the one she'd give me when I spoke of monsters under my bed and Sand Man that would come back to get me.

I wasn't a little girl though. I was sixteen.

That terrified look in a mother's features never gets easier to face. Knots eat up my stomach, and it's almost like I know before she ever speaks.

Fuck.

"Who are you talking about, Bell? Who's Ivy? What's tick tock?" she enunciates.

I ignore her poor pronunciation of the app as the breath punches from my lungs. The gift drops to the carpet with a heavy thud. Her arms pull me in as I stand stiffly in her embrace and listen to the words she coos in my ear.

"It'll be alright, hunny. It'll be alright. You're alright."

But it's not alright. Nothing is.

Because the Sand Man did come back.

Just not for me.

CHAPTER TWO

Bella

A storm that thunders through my heart flashes with lightening outside the painted glass windows. Shining, crimson eyes watch me from the shadows of the Great Hall. I'm at the center of the event. Their waiting attention presses down on me in a frantic feeling of breathlessness.

I don't want to be here.

I don't want to do this.

The arching angles of the red stained glass cast a sinister color across the tile floor. The room is painted red. My white dress is painted red.

And so are my bloody hands.

My eyes open fast while the air in my lungs burns for a full breath. I stumble out of my bed, and the moment my feet touch the cold, familiar floorboards, I know I'm okay. I'm not in that place anymore. He can't get me here.

I'm home.

The slamming of my heart doesn't slow though. Because Ivy's very much not okay.

How—how did I even get here? How did I end up in my bed?

A migraine pounds through my skull. I think through the night and the way I sat at the kitchen table with a hot cup of coffee and both of my parents staring at me like I'd fall apart right in front of them.

But that's the last thing I remember . . .

"The pills," I whisper.

White moonlight shines muted color into my childhood bedroom, but my gaze lands on the little medicine bottle on my night stand. My jaw grinds with pain at the memories of how often my mother watched to make sure I swallowed them down. When I turned eighteen, I refused to keep dosing myself like I had a sickness.

The pills stopped the dreams. It didn't stop me from remembering though.

My hand trembles as I pick the container up. The clatter of little tablets inside turns my stomach. I can't fucking believe my mother would drug me. She is always so distressed about any mention of nightmares or monsters or anything out of the ordinary at all.

I remember her! Ivy was real! She was a curly-haired, blonde baby who weighed less than my school backpack when she was born! The brightest blue eyes shined out to the world with so much innocence! She had the loudest laugh, and I wanted nothing more than to make sure she never had anything happen to her to take that happiness in her voice away!

She was real! She *is* real!

My arm flings out wildly, and the cracking of plastic shatters across the wall as the pills rain down to the floor with a rattle of bittersweet destruction. They're still rolling across the hardwood floor when I storm out of my bedroom and across the hall. The cold handle is turned with force, and the white door is flung open without a sound.

But the pink walls and the white plush comforter isn't what greets me. The flashy room that I helped her decorate isn't there anymore. Flat white walls press in on me, and the bed that was once hers has an old quilt that Grandma made thrown across it like it's ready for a guest.

"What the fuck is happening?" I hiss. I know exactly what's happening. I just have never seen it firsthand.

He made her disappear.

How? How could he erase her entire existence?

I guess I understood when it happened to me but Ivy? She was different. She's too much of a memory for anyone to forget. Especially her own mother.

Dampness stings my eyes and still I refuse to believe it. I stride through the small room and throw open the closet doors. They bang against the hinges, but . . .

Three plastic hangers sway in the vacant closet.

It's empty.

The dresses, the belts, the glitter boots, they're all gone.

My fingers fist hard into my palms, and I feel myself trembling with fury and helplessness. My head shakes back and forth.

I'm not crazy. I'm not crazy. I'm not crazy.

Once more, I search for any sign of the little girl who climbed all over me when she was a toddler and I was just a teen who'd always wanted a sibling. I was an only child for so long, I loved her the moment I saw her. Eleven years separated us, but it never mattered. She was my baby sister. And I'd always be there for her.

My feet stomp through the upstairs without care for my parents who are sleeping just one room below. Out in the darkness of the hall, I search the long walls that lead to the bathroom and the office at the end. Picture frames cascade down the space.

And vomit stings my throat when I see the picture of Iv and me in red Christmas dresses ten years ago. Except . . . I sit alone in the portrait. A big smile plastered across my face as I look to the left . . . where a shadowy spot lies empty in my father's arms.

"No," I whisper.

The family picture to the right of it is just as unsettling. So much so that I pull the thing from the wall entirely. Mom and Dad smile bright behind me. I sit in the front with a fresh pink scar across my left cheek that no one ever fully looks at. My head tilts in toward someone . . . but no one's there.

The quaking in my hands clenches around the black frame before I release it and slam it to the ground altogether. Glass kicks up around my socks, but I ignore it as I walk away. I fucking can't sit back and accept that she's gone.

I won't let her go through the torment I did. The Sand Man will never hurt her the way he did me. I won't let him!

The quietness of the house is only disturbed by the shaking of the lamp from my feet storming through my bedroom once more. Instead of preparing for bed, though, I pull my black boots on, tie my long dark hair back, and climb into bed.

There's an anger to the way I stare up at the ceiling. I used to memorize the shapes and strokes of the mundane white surface above my bed. It's something I've looked at a hundred thousand times.

But tonight, it's different.

Tonight, I summon a monster.

CHAPTER THREE

Bella

I wish I could say this is the first time I've called out to The Ruiner since I left the Kingdom of Carnal. It's not though. I've practiced to speak to him as much as I have to avoid him. He's a monster . . .

And he's my friend.

I think about his name. The way it sounds when I whisper it. The way it crawls across my tongue and leaves anticipation pulsing in my chest.

My lashes close softly against my cheeks.

Lucid dreaming isn't for the faint of heart. You have to be a real control freak to want to be in control of your life during your waking *and sleeping* hours.

I guess I'm that special of a fuck-up that I studied it for years. It has helped me avoid nightmares as much as it has helped me enter them.

The last time I did it was the last night Jonathon

came home drunk. He blamed me for not making him dinner. *At two in the morning.* He blamed me for the guy in our calc class for asking for my number. Even though I smiled and said I had a boyfriend. He just . . . he blamed me. *For everything.*

Then he punished me.

And then I called The Ruiner.

I shove out the memory of the last time I ever saw Jonathon screaming from the other side of our bed. Our blue comforter still has a tear in the corner from how hard he hung on before being ripped away.

I don't think of that. I focus.

"Ruiner," I whisper in my mind's eye, my thoughts calming sweetly. A blankness of just inky nothingness fills me. I am empty.

All is silent.

The knocking of my own heart is all that's heard as I fall into a between space of consciousness and sleep. Minutes tick by unnoticed. Maybe he won't come. He always comes though. He's the one thing stable in my life.

God knows I'm not.

I sink into the recess of my sleep even more and think about his name once more with hard concentration this time.

Ruiner.

Ruiner.

Ru—

"You should be asleep, Pretty Monster." His deep, dark voice hums through the room.

The hair along my arms lifts. It shivers through me.

Imagine having a crush on the older guy in school and never, ever admitting it. And now imagine that guy is actually a seven-and-a-half-foot-tall monster who now visits you at night.

Under your bed.

Yeah, the crush I had on him then is still alive and well, obviously.

I pull forward through the heavy curtain of sleep and slowly open my eyes as a soft smile presses to my lips. He can change my mood just like that. He's a reassurance and a blessing. A true friend.

"And you shouldn't be hiding beneath my bed, but here we are." I lie perfectly still, the smile still haunting my lips as I wait for the quiet to fade and his warm voice to calm me once more.

"Do you need me for something, Bella?" His breath kisses across my name in a more delicate tone like even my name is something he holds with care.

I swallow, and though I want to crawl under the bed and demand he take me to her, I try not to show my cards. I don't want anyone knowing how important she is to me. It's dangerous in the Kingdom of Carnal to care about someone. Those bastards will kill everyone you love just to see what breaks you.

So I can't tell Ruin. Even if he is the closest thing to a friend that I've had in a long, long time.

"I haven't seen you in years," I whisper.

It's a distraction, but it's true. He's careful not to break the rules like some monsters do. They cannot enter the mortal world. If a human comes to them, if they reach into the depths of the darkness under the bed, that's fair game. If they summon a haunting at a séance, that's fair game. Hell, if they leave the closet door open and accidently say the wrong prayer before bed, that's fair game.

But otherwise, they cannot come uninvited.

So what the hell did Ivy do to gain the attention of the Sand Man?

"I'd say the same but . . ." His velvety voice carries off like a shadow in the night, and it has me sidetracked for a moment.

"You've seen me?" I arch a brow at that, but curiosity really can kill.

"Mmm, you had a mirror on the back of your bedroom door in your apartment. It showed . . ." his throat clears roughly.

"Did you spy on me?!"

"No!"

A disbelieving silence falls in before he speaks again.

"I checked in on you from time to time. Especially when that man lived there." His voice rumbles beneath me, and it's such a relaxing sensation to feel his tone as well as hear it.

It feels safe.

The smile against my lips is bittersweet, and it only grows as he confesses his protectiveness over me.

"Thank you. For taking care of him, by the way."

His hum of a reply is short. "He tasted as disgusting as he acted."

"I believe that." I don't dwell on the specifics of how Ruiner got rid of Jonathon. He's a soul eater, but he's also . . . a mixture of monster races. I don't need to think too hard to imagine the details. I'm grateful all the same.

"Ruin," I whisper, and I swear I hear a faint groan at the sound of his name against my lips.

"Yes, Pretty Monster?" His words skim across my flesh, the hair rising across my arms like a lover's touch ghosting down my body.

"Can I see you?"

At that, hesitation settles. The weight of it presses down on me in the silence.

"Please?"

"That's a very bad idea." His tone's receding, and my fear of losing Ivy entirely rises up in my chest.

"Please, Ruiner."

"You escaped once, Bella. You won't leave a second time."

"*Please.*"

"I—I have to go."

He's saying no without actually saying no because he and I both know that he can't fucking say no to me!

My soul isn't tainted. I'm not cruel or sinful. I'd be delicious. He has said so himself a time or two.

I leap from the bed. My boots hit the floor hard with impatience, and instead of fearfully pulling back the sheet, I rip it away and reach into the heavy darkness.

You never reach under the bed.

Never.

Because a monster can't resist the smell of a human.

Especially a monster who can't resist me already.

Claws sink into the skin of my wrist. Pain tears through my flesh. Air shoves from my lungs. A slamming overtakes my frail heart. My eyes clench closed.

And then he takes me.

CHAPTER FOUR

The splinter of floorboards bites against my stomach as my shirt catches on an old nail and then a twisted, jagged tree root. Dirt scatters over my hair and eyes. My mouth clamps shut, and I try not to breathe in the cold earth as I'm pulled right through it.

The talons around my wrist are accompanied by another set of razor-sharp nails before a hard, strong chest meets mine. Everything's a mess of darkness and dust. It takes some time before it all settles around us in shining rays like glitter glinting in the sun.

But it does settle. My eyes open slowly, and those piercing bright blue eyes stare down on me. Not blue like the sea . . . blue like nature clawed its way into this man's gaze and froze his heart solid.

Singed cerulean maybe. Crystalized turquoise.

His eyes are so hypnotic, I don't immediately notice

the burning scar that's lighting up his face like lava just beneath the inky black wound.

"Wha—what happened?" My fingertips lift, and the sting of his jagged blemish burns across my fingertips. But I don't pull back.

Dark lashes close softly, and for a moment, it feels like eight long years haven't passed at all. He's cradling me in his arms. His broad shoulders and towering height shadow over me like I'm a small gem he'll always keep hidden away close to his heart. Enormous black wings cover protectively around us. Hidden beneath those wings are eight spiderlike legs. He uses them like weapons. He splits his victims open, and . . .

I blink those vicious thoughts away.

When he looks at me, it's like I'm that sixteen-year-old girl still trying to remember how to keep my weak heartbeat steady so he doesn't hear how he affects me.

Ruiner isn't generically attractive. He's bulky and scarred. A man with eight thin spider legs and massive black wings isn't typically called cute. But just beneath that calm and collected exterior is a violent man.

He's sinfully sexy. A roughness that can protect and a heart that can love only emphasize that.

And I fell right into that attraction as a young girl. Even if I never did tell him.

The sunlight shines high in the sky above the pine-scented forest. The midnight hours of my little hometown are long gone. That's not the only difference between the two places though. No, the magic that's burnt into this kingdom effects its inhabitants far more than anything else.

The darkness, they call it.

I know that firsthand. Magic crawled beneath my skin during the short year I was here. And the embered scar on my friend's body is just another symbol of the power in this world. The longer you stay, the more monstrous you become.

"Why did you do that?" he growls, showing the sharpness of his upper and lower canines. He lowers me to the mossy earth much more gently than how he speaks. "I told you not to come here!"

There's that rage that burns beneath his smooth surface.

"You didn't have to bring me." My arms cross over my chest, and it takes a second for me to notice his gaze lingering there. Unlike most people, it isn't my cherry-red birthmark he's looking at. His attention is like the flames of a fire licking along my skin.

"You're . . . different." Those words are mumbled instead of spoken with the confidence and dominance he normally has.

"So are you," I say, my attention sweeping over his black boots and pants to the veering valley of his hips, his broad shoulders, his dark beard, and midnight black wingspan. I guess that's the bonus for men who have wings: shirts are overrated.

Physically, he's the same. Brutishly handsome in a very nontypical way. A giant of a man, standing over my five-eleven frame like I'm a petite little thing. But something buried deep inside him, it's different. He was always the laughing, good-time friend. He hid his jagged side from me so well back then. And now . . .

He has been hurt.

By what? And why didn't he ever show it when he was just the mysteriously dark voice beneath my bed?

"You're up to something," he says, his gaze now searching me instead of appraising me.

"Has it not occurred to you that maybe I missed you?"

"No. Not once, actually."

I shrug.

I did though.

It's hard for me to admit that to a man, but I missed Ruiner more than I've ever missed anyone in my entire life. When I was sixteen, I could tell him anything. That's why I still whispered to him in the middle of the night years later. Even if he didn't always answer, I'd confess to him like a diary no one would ever know the contents of.

Instead of correcting him, I simply tilt my head high and stand my ground. Despite his monstrous nature, Ruiner may be the only man in my life who hasn't hurt me. He's one of the good ones. From my very first cheating boyfriend at sixteen years old, to the groping men who slip me dollar bills at *Club 45*, to the Sand Man himself, men . . . they've been complete shit to me. Maybe that's why I can't truly connect with anyone.

Especially men.

So when I show the confidence I've built up around me over the years, it doesn't waver beneath his watchful stare. I don't second-guess his intentions. He won't hurt me.

But I don't know if he'll help me either.

"I want to go to the Kingdom of Carnal."

"No," he says flatly.

"Fine." His brows lower at my instant reply. "I'll find a wild minotaur to take me. Their herds still run rogue on the outskirts of the kingdom?"

I'd never.

But he doesn't need to know that.

"Stop it." He chastises like I'm nothing more than a tantrum-throwing child.

I have news for him: my tantrum hasn't even fucking started yet, my friend. Just wait till I get my hands on that sandy dandy son of a bitch for taking my little sister!

"I'm going to the Kingdom. You can take me, or I'll figure it out myself, Ruin." I'm good at faking my self-assurance. That's the thing about dancing: never show your emotions. Only your ability to control them. I tighten my folded arms, but that poised confidence is nothing compared to the striding steps he takes toward me. Another and another and another until my own staggering footfalls hit tree bark, and I'm staring up at those wild eyes that are boring down on me. Heat flares to life between us. His temper clearly rises, and in an instant, his massive hand snatches around my jaw. Sharp, black talons slide out, biting at tender flesh.

"*Do not* go there, Bella. You're going to listen to me, and you're going to pay-fucking-attention when I say you're going home!"

His snapping canines are so close to me, I can feel his breath against my lips. And it's then that he too realizes his mistake: *Simply, being close to me.*

Heavy inhales wave across my flesh, turning from furious to curious. His mouth closes without a sound. The dark center of his gaze takes over the pretty blue as he fixates on one thing and one thing only: my scent. Sharp talons hold me in place, the points piercing the skin along my throat and jawline. Black lashes flutter slowly as a long inhale breathes me in. A light sensation flutters along my neck with his every breath. His head tilts low. Smooth skin brushes from the low curve of my neck all the way up behind my ear, his warm breath washing over me as he takes me in.

I was trained by the Sand Man himself. After that, I practiced defense fighting for eight long years at a gym on the South Side of Chicago. I could get out of Ruiner's clutches if I wanted . . . if my lusty brain worked well enough to think about anything but how nice it'd feel if he tore off my panties with those sharp teeth of his. In this moment, my panties are malfunctioning and taking control of my rational thoughts.

Panties . . . they don't make good life choices, that's for sure.

"I've watched you for years. I hear your voice in my dreams even, and yet . . . how could I not know how fucking delectable you smell, Bella?" His voice rasps over my name this time in that darkly intimate tone that shivers all through me.

I shift in his hold, and as my lashes flutter, I find my palms lightly pressing over his chest, feeling the heavy pulse of his heartbeat just beneath my fingertips. As well as that burning scar that etches down his pectoral. My hips shift beneath his weight, and it only makes things worse for my panty-controlled brain.

"Ruin," I shakily whisper. "I *need* to go to the Kingdom. I can't tell you why. But I need to." My eyes clench closed, and I can't stop the emotion trembling my voice. "*Please.*"

The drumming of our hearts beating against one another passes the time. Somehow, my heart is as strong as his in this moment. His presence has the ability to make me stronger, it seems. Our words might not fit together well, but our bodies definitely do. We weren't like this before. Before, I was just a kid, and he was just a friend I was lucky enough to find in my darkest moment.

But now—it's entirely different now. His hand against my neck isn't controlling suddenly. It's caressing. My temple leans into his, and I almost don't want him to answer me. Because the moment he speaks, the spell we're clearly under in this moment will be broken.

I won't admit it, but I like the way he feels. I love the safety of his body and the warmth of his skin seeping into mine. He feels good.

So fucking g—

He steps back abruptly. Once a large gap of space is between him and me, a coldness wafts over my flesh where his body heat seeped into mine. He takes a deep breath, shakes his head, and swallows.

"Stay by me. Don't draw attention to yourself. And we won't stay long. I don't want you here after sundown."

A smile overtakes my features as I look up at the monstrous man, ignoring the warning of the dangers of staying in this chaotic kingdom at dark. The magic that crawls out when the sun set is named the Darkness for a reason. If that sinister title isn't warning enough, I don't know what is.

I nod.

"Agreed?"

"Agreed!" I say immediately.

But truthfully, I'll stay as long as it takes. I care about Ivy's life more than my own. I don't want to face the Sand Man, but I will.

I just can't tell my only friend that.

CHAPTER FIVE

Bella

We trek quietly through the forest for somewhere around an hour. It's a guess, but I'm good at telling time, honestly. Whether it's the estimate of a single hip-swaying song or the time it takes a man to get drunk, time is easy to tell for those who are observant enough to see it.

The silence of nature isn't something I've heard in a while though. It's nice to soak it in. The occasional scramble of little feet along rough tree bark breaks up my thoughts. It's the cracking of large branches beneath Ruiner's boots that speak the loudest of all.

I eye him subtly as we walk. His features remain like an unwritten book: all blank pages and spilled ink of words not yet spoken. But his body language, it's screaming.

Screaming STAY THE FUCK AWAY.

"What happened after I left?" It's the first words I've dared to say, but it's all I've thought about since the moment I landed in his arms.

What happened to him?

His broad shoulders lift carelessly, his wings rising to show the sleek black hint of a spider-like leg beneath.

"The same as when you were here. King Leavon continued searching for his Carnal Queen of dark power." He exhales heavily on that title, and even I wince at the memory of how hard Leavon wanted me to be her. It isn't often the Sand Man doesn't get what he wants. But he didn't get me. "And I . . . fucking got away from it all. Got away from him."

"You resigned from The Brotherhood?"

A snort hums through him. "Something like that."

The Brotherhood is the highest rank anyone could ask for. It's the King's chosen council and a vital part of the Kingdom's hierarchy. To be brothers with the king is an honor.

I narrow my eyes at the evasive man on my left.

"Did he—" I pause because I was really hoping he'd tell me. But it looks like he's going to make me tear the truth out of him. Bit by bit. "Did the Sand Man give you that scar?"

Scar doesn't feel like the right word for such a jagged, ripping wound that stretches across the full side of his jaw, neck, shoulder, and torso.

That veil of mystery that covers his serious face doesn't waver. He nods only once.

As he holds back a tangle of vines for me to pass through. The thickness of the forest slips away along with the many, many questions on the tip of my tongue. In the distance, hints of dark rooftops scatter along the horizon. And the golden peak of the Castle of Carnal gleams in the pristine sunlight.

The deep blue of the sea curls around the city like the water itself is lifting the kingdom higher.

I can smell the salty sea. I can hear a ripping waterfall somewhere in the distance. So much beauty is here in the tainted darkness of this city.

The questions of Ruiner's scar, my past and his, and everything in between fall away as so many foul memories slam into me. Sometimes all I am is memories. And I hate that this place is reminding me of that. The breath leaves my lungs entirely.

It's Ruiner's growling voice that breaks the trance.

"Fuck off! She's not for sale!" His big hands shoo aggressively at a group just a few yards away that I hadn't even noticed. "She's not property. Advert your fucking beady-goat eyes off of her!"

Half a dozen men stare at me with enlarged, glossy orbs. Their long manes of hair are matted and disheveled, and the unsettling, hungry look in the gazes is far stranger than the fact that they're standing on beastly, bullish legs. A minotaur from the back yells something at Ruiner, but the braying sound of it gets lost in translation.

I don't lower my attention. I don't cower. Weakness

will never be shown. Even if their stare feels like it's peeling back and crawling under my flesh with each passing second. A large hand falls gently to the small of my back. Ruin herds me away like I'm a sweet little lamb in a field of horny bulls.

The female populace among minotaur is nearly nonexistent. They're a dying breed. And the forceful way they breed, that explains their fresh-meat stares entirely.

Even after we've followed the dirt path down the hill and have many yards separating us, Ruiner still glares back with that stony look of brutal aggression. I have no doubt he'd rip a man (or monster) limb from limb for me.

The night the rain was so cold it chilled me to the bone shivers over my skin like it was just yesterday. The rain had drenched my hair clean, but it couldn't wash the blood from my gown. I came right to him. I threw open the door to his one-room cottage. Ruiner had looked at me then with big, astonished eyes and saw what I see in him every day: vehemence. He just didn't know I was capable of it. And honestly, neither did I until that night.

A farm animal sound shakes through the quiet. It's a ridiculous sound . . . but it seems it's a threat.

Ruiner stops first, his spine going ramrod straight as he looks up at the two hooves standing in our path.

"What's a fu-kar like you doing with a l-aaaaady

like 'er?" The minotaur's hooves waft dirt around his heavy steps.

A storm of thunderous footfalls follow suit, their stride mimicking the pounding of my heart. More of them step out from the brush lining the cliff near the sea. There are suddenly dozens of them now. All men. All towering over myself as well as Ruiner with their wild eyes boring down on us.

"*Bella*," Ruiner whispers, his big hand coming up to push me quietly behind his wingspan.

"Yeah?" I ask just as carefully hushed.

Anticipation fills my chest. Seconds are counted by the hammering of my heart.

"*Run.*"

And then he's lunging at them. Leather wings spread wide, releasing the eight legs held beneath. The long, black tendons uncurl one by one. Ruiner lifts up, his wings raising him high before he swoops down on the man who insulted him. The points of his spider legs slide right through the minotaur's torso. He's drawn up above Ruiner, his hooves kicking out to aid him.

Two others rush my friend. And then four. And then seven. And then there are too many surrounding him to even see the bloody display or the tips of Ruiner's glorious wings at all. I run. Just not as Ruiner wanted me to.

I run to him. My hands grip the coarse hair of someone's back. My boot leverages against him there

too. And then I'm standing, teetering up atop the minotaur's back as he hunches down for me.

There's a split second among the chaos where
Ruiner's furious gaze slides to me. And though I can't
hear him, I know exactly what he says.

"Motherfucker!"

And then I leap into the center of the mass
destruction.

The magic here, the darkness, it once gave me a
very special skill. I just have to—a braying man elbows
my ear as he slams his fist into Ruiner's jaw, not even
remotely aware of the woman he said he wanted less
than five minutes ago.

Jesus. This is why you assholes can't have anything
nice!

I just have to hold eye contact with my assailan . . .
assailants.

Shit. There are too many of them. I don't even
think I remember how to use the magic . . .

"Can I just," I try to look into the man's eyes closest
to me, but he's just shoving forward to get closer to the
dozens of others surrounding Ruiner.

Seriously, this is just overkill at this point. He can't
let all of you kill him! Make some fucking space.

I jar my own elbow into the man nearest me, and
the animal-like wheeze that startles through him is the
only evidence that I did any damage at all. Arms and
hooves and legs and breath are all over me, sickening
me from the throng of men I'm now stuck in.

"WHY—" a growling familiar voice says. "Don't you ever listen to me?" Ruiner spews, slamming his fist into a face, or a stomach, or possibly a man, I'm not even sure at this point.

"Sorry, I can't hear you over the many compliments of my adoring fans," I snark, being completely shoved aside and tossed out of the throng entirely. I lift my hands at the total lack of intelligence happening before me. "I don't know if I've ever been this insulted to not be hit on by a guy before. Like I get it. He's a spider bat man. That's like super impressive to men, I'm sure." I tap my boot restlessly and try to figure out how to get these asshats off of my friend. "But I have these," I yell loudly, lifting my thin black shirt and . . .

Flashing the crowd of minotaurs.

Yeah. I've hit a new low in life, I think.

The braying, the shoving, the bloody riot all halts at once. Dozens of big, glossy orbs look my way. Silent appreciation flutters in.

Somewhere in those empty, bullish heads of theirs, there's a chant happening. I can almost hear it, I swear.

Boobs. Boobs. Booooooobs.

Apparently, you don't need dark magic to solve problems. You just need breasts.

A cocky smirk touches my lips.

Until they all push off of Ruiner and slowly stalk my way.

"Bella! Run!" Ruiner tells me once more.

And this time, I fucking listen.

Weak heart, don't fail me now.

My legs never stop. The dirt of the path down to the city is long gone, and only the softest green grass slips against my boots as I thrash to run faster and faster. The rushing of water becomes louder and louder. It all flits by in a panic as the herd's screams ring in my ears. A hand grips my arm. The minotaur's nails dig into my flesh.

And then I jump.

His hold on me disappears as cold wind catches my hair. The salty smell of the sea fills my senses like a wave of relief. Only to be drowned in its depths when I crash headfirst into the water. It feels as though nails are spraying into my face. It soaks right into me: the sound of it fills my ears like the sting of it fills my nostrils.

With thrashing arms, my desperation carries me through the darkness. I can't make out up or down, but I'll try anyway. I'll never stop trying.

Even if my lungs are burning with each slow second that slips by.

It all starts to press down on me. I can't reach the surface. I can't hold my breath any longer.

It's too much.

Strong arms catch my waist, and I'm hauled into his embrace. I'm pulled through the weight of the waves. It feels euphoric and terrifying all at the same time.

My head lifts from the water with a rattling gasp of air hitting my throat with painful intakes. With heavy kicks and uneven strokes, I keep myself above the push and pull of the current.

"Bella! Bella!" my savior calls.

Ruin's dark lashes are lined with dampness, making his piercing eyes seem like the ocean itself is looking at me with such intensity.

He's so fucking gorgeous. I—

"Bella, I can't fucking swim!"

Shit.

His wings flick against the water, but the shape of them catches the water like a bowl at the center. His body isn't made for this.

And I have no damn idea how I'm supposed to rescue a giant of a man like The Ruiner.

"It's okay. It's okay," I tell him. I say it over and over again. I slide my arm around his slick torso, his wings jarring into my every stroke as I head toward the shore.

But it's so far away.

"It's okay," I tell the both of us.

I reassure myself as much as I do him. I say it to keep morale. I say it—I say it because the sea is pulling me back with every inch I gain.

It's impossible.

And still, I keep going. Ruiner has saved me more times than he even knows.

I won't fail him.

My eyes aren't even open when jagged coral cuts into my arms. I fling at the sea. My poor attempt to keep swimming is just engraved into my brain, even as my tired limbs start to give out.

It feels like broken glass along my knees. My palms splay out to hold myself up from the unseen sharpness, but pain slashes across my flesh there too.

Until I'm scooped up. My dark hair covers my face. I'm too tired to even try to blow a breath of air at the veil of wet, messy locks blinding my sight.

"It's okay," Ruin whispers sweetly to me on that crushed velvet voice of his.

My head jostles into his shoulder when his knees hit the ground. His protective hold never releases me as he slowly lowers to the grass. Through my tangled hair, I see his lashes close, his ragged breaths turning slow and even finally.

He leapt into the sea to save me. He knew his wings would sink him, and yet he leapt after me anyway.

Why does his near-death experience feel all warm and fuzzy inside my chest?

His strong heartbeat settles into a steady rhythm that fills my ears as I lean into his smooth chest. It's easy to fall into him and curl up in his big arms. There was never a problem with finding comfort in my friend. There was only the problem of remembering just that: my strong, gorgeous protector . . . is just a friend.

CHAPTER SIX

It takes hours to find our way back. It's a journey to travel from the sea up to the highest point of the kingdom. Dense silence carries on for so long, our little dirt path widens to smooth cobblestone streets. The Kingdom of Carnal soon comes alive all around me, and I still can't help but peer around at the buildings that hang lanterns at each door. This strange world is notorious as a refuge for Monsters. Other creatures, the prettier ones like the Fae kingdom to the north, they don't welcome the broken the way that Carnal does. Anyone strange and bizarre, they're welcome here with open arms.

And they're created here too.

The parasitic magic of this kingdom that sinks into your bones and infects your flesh, that's the price you pay for acceptance.

An old woman with a tattered, graying shawl fills a

baby carriage with knickknacks. Old clocks, vases, figurines, and rusting tins fill the pale blue stroller to the brim. We pass her by on the wide-open street, and her graying eyes fill with white smoke as she looks up at me, pinning me in place with the weight of her stare.

"Care for a souvenir, Pretty Girl?" Her talon-like hand reaches out to me, and in the palm of her lined hand rests a silver ring with an opal gem at the center.

"I've seen that ring before," I mutter as I stand transfixed, staring at the jewelry as dozens of others pass me by.

That's Ivy's ring. I gave it to her for her birthday last year.

My fingers lift one at a time as I reach for the memento in the flat of the old woman's palm.

And then something hard stings across my knuckles before I ever make contact.

"What the fuck!" I glare up at my friend at my side. Before he can explain the slap he just gave my hand, he's ushering me away from that side of the street entirely.

"Don't talk to strangers, Bella. That's Monster's law 101."

"That was Ivy's ring! She has seen Ivy!" I turn to haul back to the woman, but I spot her tossing a piece of paper trash to the ground before dusting her hands off and setting her sights on a young girl with a burlap sack positioned over her head entirely, hiding her

44

features from everyone. That doesn't stop the old woman.

"Care for a souvenir, Pretty Girl?" she repeats.

The eerie girl in the burlap sack doesn't even pause or acknowledge the woman as she quickly passes by.

The woman shakes her head and tries again on the next man with a horn protruding through the center of his forehead.

. . . she's a hustler.

She never had Ivy's ring at all. It's simple trans-fixion magic. I learned to do it my first month here. If you say something with enough conviction, you can change the way someone thinks. And even the way they see. A little bit of magic and a whole lot of confidence is all someone needs for transfixion.

I shake my head and remind myself not to trust anyone here. Even if it comes to my little sister. Always lead with doubt in the Kingdom of Carnal.

I follow closely at Ruiner's side, and his attention slides to me out of the corner of his eye every two to five seconds. The crowd thickens, and the tension lining his back tightens. Every muscle in his body is taut and ready. The heart of the city just outside the king's castle is the worst of Carnal. A poor kingdom made entirely of outcasts aren't always the kindest citizens.

It isn't until the small, circular cottages come into view that the thousands of people brushing against me start to calm into just a trickle of passersby. The cottages are spaced out largely just outside a towering brick wall that reaches high above the little one-room houses that line a circle around the castle walls. I remember this area fondly.

Because this is the Brotherhood's homes. And I stayed in the one nearest to the gate for the first few days I arrived in Carnal. The Ruiner's cottage.

The kingdom's one hope is that the king will find his Chosen bride. It's foretold that a match of magic will bring great power as well as great wealth to the Kingdom of Carnal. And so, every year, King Leavon steals away six women (I use the term women loosely considering my baby sister is only thirteen fucking years old). And as a help, the Brotherhood, too, steals a single girl each. A total of ten are brought into the kingdom. And over the last hundred years, none have lived past that one year of initiation. Except for me: *the one who got away.*

Golden gates line the entrance to a smooth sidewalk. The narrow metal bars don't hide the castle's grandeur. It spreads far across green grass like an infection seeping into the lawn. The mere sight of the sleek white brick estate turns my stomach.

I swore I'd never come back to this shiny shithole of insanity. But if she's here, I'll never leave until I know she's safe.

For several seconds, I don't move. Then I see her. With just a few steps, I enter. I stand with my back to the glittering gates. My gaze spans the sweeping will-o'-the-wisps that dance in the breeze. Their flowers glow a

OF SINS AND PSYCHOS

ruby red from each thin branch that dusts the whirling, swirling walkway. The monstrous doors once looked like a happily-ever-after awaiting my young future as I gazed up at the golden paint that framed the entrance doors.

Now it looks like a snarling mouth ready to eat my little sister alive.

Pale blonde hair, the very opposite of my own, sways around her face. Sharp angles and full lips always made everyone stop and stare. At just thirteen years old, she brings in friends by the dozens with her pretty smile alone. But a dark part of her, one she doesn't even know exists yet, will sneak out once the sun goes down in this world.

In approximately four minutes, by my count. I peer up at the skies and make note of the warm haze burning along the horizon.

A long breath of nerves shoves from my lungs.

"It's getting dark," Ruiner murmurs. "We wasted too much time. We have to go, Bella,"

I take another careful step into the courtyard. If I just remind her what she left at home, I can get her to come with me. I don't understand what would make her leave in the first place, but if she sees me, I know she'll come home with me. And I can go back to pretending I don't think about the Sand Man twice a day, every day.

My attention zeros in when her big blue eyes flash with a shadow of darkness.

Shit.

The Kingdom of Carnal isn't just a kingdom of Monsters. It creates them. The longer you're here, the worse it becomes. Night by night, you lose your sense of humanity. It festers.

It creates chaos.

I shake my head as my own darkness rattles within me.

"Bella," Ruin says from somewhere in the distance of my racing thoughts.

I glance away to the others. Ten of them are Chosen women. The rest, they're courtiers. But not. In a way, they're slaves to one master. A man I ran away from but can never truly escape.

The proof of that is in the fact that I stand here in his kingdom once again. And I hate that it feels like I never left. I hate that the need to appease him is growing wilder in my chest with each slipping hint of the orange sunlight casting across his beautiful, glowing castle.

Two minutes.

With a black hair tie, I pull my dark hair up higher on my head. If I don't, the darkness will only leave the long locks in a tangled nest once I wake in the morning.

Ivy pushes her blonde hair behind her ear, and if we came here as friends looking for adventure, I'd tell her to pull it back into a tight bun. Maybe I'd warn her not to wear nice skirts like the one that's blowing in the breeze now. Maybe I'd tell her not to get too close to the one man everyone here idolizes.

My fingers lift, and absently, I skim over the scar that lines the side of my face, the one my hair hides so easily. It shows very clearly now. But I'd rather show the ugly memory than deal with two days' worth of ratty tangles.

One minute.

I stride toward her on large, rushing steps. I hear my name called over and over again on a hushed, angry tone, but I have to get to her.

Now.

Ink swirls in her eyes as I'm sure it does in my own. And the urge of the darkness inside turns her alluring smile into a leer. Bad decisions and deadly ideas are slashing through her pretty mind's eye. It's written all over her innocent face.

"Shit," I hiss as I see the chaotic thing surfacing from within her.

I stumble up the steps, and when her eyes meet mine, a warm sensation of relief blooms within me.

"Ivy!" I say on a long exhale.

Her pretty face tilts slightly, and once more, alarm bells ring at the back of my mind, but I shut the window on the sound and take her hand in mine.

"Ivy, I—I don't know why you're here but—"

"Do I know you?" She smiles, and it's only mini-mally eerie with the wells of blackness in her gaze.

Does she know me . . .

I blink at her.

What—What has he done? What did he do to her?

"I—"

A man strides up the few steps and stops before her, stealing away all of her attention with a handsome smile like the devil himself. Two black horns twist up from his pale hair, giving him a height no one can ignore. His messy locks hide his features from me, but the simple crowd of wide-eyed awaiting Carnals just behind him tells me all I need to know.

Initiation night.

I'm pushed back, staggering down the two steps, and I lose sight of her all together. The throng of people around me shifts. Dozens of arms brush by me, and I try to keep sight of her blonde head of hair in the crowd.

The Chosen, my sister included, abandon the steps of the castle and trail behind the cackles and howls of their elder Carnals. What will they do to them? How will they spark the wildness of the new audience who haven't yet explored this chaotic kingdom?

Whatever it is, Ivy isn't ready.

I take a single step before sharp nails dig into my upper arm.

"We're going," Ruiner seethes out.

A manic sensation tells me to laugh in his face. There's an asinine urge to tackle his enormous body to the ground and shake my ass in his face until he submits to my erratic authority. I shove my hands down my face and try to get a fucking grip. I've got to keep control in this kingdom.

If I don't, Ivy will pay the price.

"I just—"

My excuse slips out while someone else slips in. A slender man with eyes as white as his hair. A smile like jagged ice cuts up his lips, and he beams it directly at Ruiner.

"Did you think you could come back to the Kingdom of Carnal and my Lord wouldn't know about it, Ruiner? The Brotherhood has missed you, my friend." His hands are folded neatly behind his very narrow back, his posture stiff and formal. "The Sand Man has requested your presence."

Ruiner's jaw twitches hard, and he glances at me out of the corner of his cold blue eyes.

He can't take me with him. He'll never bring me back to the man I outran so long ago.

The strong hand wrapped around my bicep slides away slowly. It skims down my arm with just enough warmth and apprehension that it sends shivers racing after the final brush of his fingertips against my wrist.

Then he walks away.

To the naked eye, I mean nothing to the batlike man striding up the castle steps without a second glance my way. We're two strangers who share a once upon a time together.

Once upon a time, we shared a bond of fear and friendship. The night he helped me escape this black hole of a kingdom was the night I believed soul mates might mean something different than what Disney has always led little girls to believe. A soul mate isn't a fleeting lover. It's a lifelong friend.

Knowing Ruin will always find me, I round the corner of the castle. I have his protection, but I don't depend on him as deeply as I once did. I'm ready this time. The night does fall, though. And the dark magic of this kingdom falls even harder. My mind feels heavy and cloudy. I'm a jumble of thoughts, as are my steps as I slip into the mass of people. My attention scans each face until I barely spot her up ahead.

She's so small. I keep several yards of space between us as the shadows settle with the fading sun, and somehow the petite frame of her shoulders seems less like a girl on the verge of womanhood and more like the little girl I left behind when I went off to Chicago. An obscure restlessness tremors within me, but I calm its energy with my own as the crowd of dozens swallows me up, and we walk farther behind the east wing of the building. Torches light up the white brick of the grand hall that sits in the shadow of the king's castle. We pass the familiar building and keep going, though.

Each deep inhale is accounted for along with each forceful exhale. I just have to focus on my breathing, and my mind will stay with me.

The magic of this place, it preys on the newcomers. It eats their naiveness alive. The wiser, the ones who have trained here, we know we have to keep ahold of what's real.

Just focus on your breathing. Focus on your breathing. Focus—

As hard as I try, the darkness keeps pulling away at my sanity.

Laughter crackles through the night, and I find myself smiling at it as well. Excitement blooms in my chest.

It's all a memory coming to life. The countless times I've revisited this place in my mind are nothing compared to the cold wind that skims over my flesh and beckons me deeper into the madness. It's freeing. It's addicting.

It's fucking intoxicating.

My boots slam over the damp grass, and I'm full-on running. I pass face after face, and none of them give me a second glance. Because they're sprinting into the wilderness of the night as well. Like animals, we flock on into the unknown with an anticipation and need for the darkness to swallow us up entirely.

Take me in and never give me back to that cruel, cruel reality.

Fuck reality.

And then the darkness sprays out with glinting embers that shoot into the night all around us like our own personal stars streaking across the heavens. A sound like gears grinding churns, and then more light blooms before my eyes in beautiful, swirling colors of gold.

A sort of carousel turns slowly, its platform void of any metal toys for children to play on. But beasts with great black wings and sturdy, dark hooves pound into the metal flooring, demanding to fly free and find the excitement of the night just as we have.

"Falhorns!" an older girl screeches with a bubble of laughter that mirrors in my chest and casts out into the whipping breeze.

"Is it a carousel?" a girl just a few feet from my sister asks.

"These are the king's creatures. The flight station assists the Falhorns with gaining momentum," a boy with unruly dark hair tells us. "It spins faster and faster, and when they're released, they spin out into thin air. They disappear, traveling through cities and kingdoms with a speed only their magic is capable of."

My lips spread wide at the beautiful sight of the demonic horses in their flight stations. They're hell-sent if I remember right. Every inch of them from their glistening hair to their big eyes is like a shadow dipped in a well of sin. Beautiful and yet . . . unnerving at the same time. Between their spiraling, dark horns is a gleaming, golden rod that ties them to the carousel. Those rods are staggered throughout. Six Falhorns are tied to the now quick-spinning platform, while the other dozens of poles are empty . . .

And it becomes very clear what initiation night

involves.

With an excited leap, my heart soars, and my hand grips the nearest pole. I'm jerked forward, my body trailing as the carousel turns rapidly. Blurs of lights and screams are all around me, and I feel . . .

Untouchable.

Once more, I leap to my feet with a cool breath of fresh air in my lungs. What I find though, is that the party has already begun.

"You a Carnal?" the man asks as he picks up a lock of my sister's long blonde hair and seems to inspect its softness between his thumb and index finger.

"Yes," she breathes out with awe and admiration.

He's the same man who led them all here. He's clearly a ringleader of some sort. And he clearly wants to put my sister in a bad, bad situation.

Her big, darkened eyes mirror the lights glinting all around us as she nods with a devious smile.

My soul itself shakes with worry for her.

She's too young. Too small. Too fragile.

Focus on your breathing, a manic reminder urges from deep at the back of my mind. But the words fade away before I ever fully process them.

"Let's prove it," the tall, beautiful, and destructive man calls out to a heckling crowd.

The way he walks alone is like a predator. He walks with the threatening grace of a jackal circling its prey. His ebony horns are demonic in appearance, but he doesn't seem like a demon. He's too pretty.

What are you?

I take a step forward to confront him. The fear slamming through my chest is what really gets me moving. I'm hurdling up and catching the nearest bar with a resounding screech that carries on through the night as I leap from one to the other to the other until I'm as high up as the pretty golden mechanics will allow me. And then I lean out, my boots nearly flat against the side of the pole as I crane myself over the watchful Carnals.

The nights I danced nearly naked for filthier men than these beasts have all led me here, huh? I guess the saying is true: if you work hard at your job, it'll pay off eventually.

"Maybe you should prove it yourself." I smile down at the man who now has his attention and sights fully on me. Ivy stands behind him. Forgotten. Safe. "Who the hell are you to decide who has to perform for us tonight?!" Laughter and cheers support my words, and I can't help but smile even more. With that, I spring out to a new bar as effortlessly as an animal swinging through vines. At the last moment, I swirl around the pretty pole and arch my back hard as I look at him upside down.

I wasn't prepared for my lungs to forget how to function though. The most alluring black eyes shimmer with a bright glint of gray shining within. A galaxy of beauty shines in the depths there.

My boot squeaks as I nearly lose my footing from

the rod I'm anchoring myself to. The muscles of my right arm are strung with a nice tension from how far out I hold myself. Long black hair hangs like a thick rope from my hair tie. I feel like a black widow ready to quietly descend down upon this riotous man.

I'd eat this fucker whole for picking on my little sister.

"And who," his hand lifts high and with one long finger, he strokes the edge of my jaw, "are you?"

"Come play and find out," I whisper, my smile sharpening viciously at the corners.

This is what I have to do to divert bad, bad things from happening to her. It's no trouble. The opposite, really. My dark little heart loves it right now. She loves the thrill of possibilities.

Breathe, I'm reminded.

And I remind that reminder to fuck right off.

Jesus. My voice of reason is a real fun-times-cock-block tonight.

The stranger's own amusement shines in his starry eyes. Eyes no monster has any right to have—like a little bit of heaven has found its way into hell . . . The spiraling, black horns peeking through his messy, pale hair are a proven point of that.

"Come down." It isn't a request. It's a cruelly laced command.

Once more, my heart leaps with excitement. *Will we fight? Fuck? Both? No one knows. And that's the entire appeal of it, isn't it?*

Sigh.

Maybe it'll be romance. Or maybe it'll be murder. But either way, my heart will be pounding in the end.

My fingers loosen, and casually, I slide down the pole. The gaze that narrows on me is still playful. Still mischievous.

But darker.

"Tie her up," he says on a rumbling bark.

My lashes flutter as my eyes widen. A gasp carries round and round and round. Nervous, excited laughter chases after it. Some Carnals have the good sense to step back from the crowd that's now closing in on me. Some leap off of the carousel entirely, choosing not to partake in whatever the midnight hour will bring. Ivy is one of the smart ones.

And that's the only calm that eases my nerves.

My gaze doesn't focus on her, but I see her all the same. I don't draw attention her way as she scurries off of the spinning platform with two other girls at her side.

And I've done what I came here to do: protect her.

Too bad I've screwed myself in the process.

Ah, well. Such is life: a constant fuck hole I somehow always manage to crawl out of.

Two men grip each of my arms, and though I don't struggle . . . they really put an effort into jerking my hands above my head.

"Needed two of you to do this, huh? One to lift each hand?" They ignore me. The two press in on me with their smooth chests as they lift me even higher, my feet dangling as the tips of my boots barely scuff the metal flooring. "You're really far too close for what's considered proper for a single lady like myself." Dude on my left just grunts as his pec squishes in on my cheek once more.

My tongue slips out, and quick as a wink, I lick him there like a deranged frog that mistakes pert nipples for flies.

His big body tenses all over before he stops his work and slowly looks down at my tilting smirk.

"Did you just . . . *lick* me?" With the lightest brush of his palm, he wipes his nipple haphazardly like that'll really fix the germs.

"Sorry, was that indecent for this situation? I wasn't provided with many rules before we started the game." I blink up at him with a heavy seriousness, and he awkwardly looks to his buddy who's still roughly tying my hands as high as he can reach. The rope bites into my wrists hard when my weight fully gives in, and neither of them mention the licking incident again as they step back.

"I get her first," a man says with white spikes framing his skull. His tongue is as white as his skin and eyes. It's an appearance of frost kissing his flesh. A jagged scar that arches from his shaved head to the middle of his chin only tells me that no one here will challenge his claim.

I mean . . . except for me.

"You're not even in line!" I roll my eyes at him. "Do you have no time management skills? Get in a single file line, and we will all get through this as quickly as possible . . ." I pause then as a new process flits through my mind. "Or should we go biggest to smallest . . ."

The crowd has grown silent, and several of the men are now openly passing nervous glances at one another.

"Drop 'em, boys and we'll settle who is to go first." The confidence ringing thorough my manic voice isn't at all like the nerves that's skittering around at the back of my mind. The darkness in this world changes us entirely. I'm not that girl calculating which man in my life might hurt me at any given minute. I'm a girl who wants—no—*deserves* respect as well as revenge when it comes to the opposite sex.

I eye them one by one, but they only shift awkwardly.

Sure. Sure. Everyone wants to use their dick, but no one wants to slap it out and show me what we're working with.

Typical.

"Never mind. A line is fine. Single file." I jerk my head at old Scar Skull as if to indicate where the front of the line obviously is, but no one dares come closer to me as if my crazy might be contagious.

It is. All crazy is contagious. One person wakes up one day and decides that normal doesn't really fit them very well. And they all realize how mundane normal really is. Out with the old and . . . in with the crazy.

"You're a strange one," the beautiful man with the cosmos eyes whispers in the silence.

"Thank you." My sultry wink only makes his smirk grow wilder.

"Take her boots off," Starry Eyes commands.

The two brutes from earlier stride toward me, but the one who's nipple I maimed so cruelly with my tongue keeps his distance. He tugs off my boot and tosses it somewhere behind me. The hard bang of the metal floor is the only indication where my dirty boots now reside.

"Pants too," Starry Eyes adds.

"Ooo," I taunt without making a sound across my invisible ohs.

Because deep inside, past my deranged mind, is logic. And logic tells me that something very, very bad is about to happen to me. My stomach turns sickly as I continue to tilt my head this way and that, swaying my hips to the soundless song that is spinning right round in my thoughts.

Taut Nips is the lucky bastard that strips off my tight leggings.

"It's harder than it looks, huh?" I ask as he struggles with the tight material at my thighs. "I'm just happy someone else has to deal with them today instead of me." I fake my confidence. My hands strain with pain along my wrists as he jerks them all the way down. "Had to lie flat on the bed this morning just to wiggle them on. Not easy being a whole snack sometimes, is it?" I smile at his glare and shake my head at his lack of decent conversation skills as he chucks my pants somewhere to join my lost boots.

The platform turns. As does my stomach.

The mantra of "just breathe" is really too little too late at this point, and my rational mind is telling me to brace myself for the worst.

But I already survived the worst. And that's how I know I can survive this.

I stand, strung up in nothing more than my black panties and black cotton crop top. It crosses the back of my mind that the few thin pieces of fabric I'm wearing can easily be taken away from me.

Everything I have can be easily taken away.

The Sand Man proved that to me years ago.

The night is a passing blur behind the man who appears more like a fallen angel than a monster. The dark smile on his lips isn't angelic though. His footfalls are soundless as he takes the space between us. He claims it all. Until the edge of his boot is skimming my glossy black painted toes. My neck angles up at him as his breath crashes down on me. His unkempt hair veils above us while he studies me. Only the edge of his thumb brushes my skin, skimming along my bottom lip. My teeth drag over the spot his digit barely touched.

The light feel of him is firing all my senses at once. My tongue rolls across my lip, and I swear I can taste his touch. My breath catches on the crisp air where he once was. It's an addiction now.

I have no idea why.

"Who are you?" he whispers like a confession of love between us.

My smile tilts hard.

"I'm the girl you shouldn't have fucked with," I whisper right back to him, my humming laughter crawling up all around me.

A strong hand snatches around my throat, and those starry eyes turn black. The light glints of silver snuff out into deep, inky wells of total chaotic sin. He turns my chin to one side as his lips ghost down the curve of my neck before hovering over my ear.

"You're bad for your own health." His whispered words dance across my flesh, raising goosebumps in their wake.

And he's right. Damn, is he right.

But I can't speak. I can't breathe. I try not to struggle. I try desperately not to make a single sound. Until it's all too much, and the choking of my own distress sputters across my lips. My lashes flutter as I try to make hard eye contact with the most beautiful gaze I've ever seen. If I can just hold his attention, my magic will come out.

I hope.

His fingers tense against my throat little by little, his frame leaning in nice and close. The softness of his lips brushes along my cheek as he speaks.

"You think this place is all a game of fun. It's not. You're nothing more than a captive to the King." His breath fans across my jaw as his grip turns painful and spotting behind my eyelids. "You're ours to play with like a pretty toy. And I'm about to make you remember that."

The rigid tightness of his palm releases suddenly. Air swoops down my throat in big gulps. Then the roughness of that palm is trailing down my shoulder. The heat of his hands can be felt near the curves of my breasts as he toys with the collar of my shirt.

"If you were smart, you'd watch your mouth around us. You could say nothing, and I'd walk away, take these Carnals with me, and just leave you stranded here like a half-naked joke to be seen in the morning."

"That's a terrible joke," I say rather breathlessly.

"But you just can't help yourself."

My head tilts at his challenge. Is this his misogynistic way of telling me I should just shut up?

Yes! The little logical voice at the back of my crumpled mind yells. *Shut. The. Fuck. Up.*

"Why would I help myself when I have you to take care of me?" I look up at him through thick, innocent lashes, my magic bubbling within me with each passing second.

But then he looks away. His head shakes slowly like a disappointed father . . . Daddy. Sorry. Daddy?

Jesus Christ, stop it!

He holds my stare once more. My magic is forgotten as heat flashes between us in tingles of nerves and anticipation. Because that's all my fragile heart ever wanted in this hellhole: the excitement of the unknown. An adventure. A love to outshine all lust.

Or maybe I'm just simply crazy.

The press of his smooth chest against mine is a buzz of adrenaline that spirals deeper inside me as his hands slide down to my hips. His head lowers. His wicked eyes shift across my features, skimming right over my birthmark and pink scar like my eyes and my lips are the most captivating part of me.

My thighs brush as I unsteadily shift from one foot to the other. My body is strung up before him like an idol ready for worship. Time sparks with everything we put into this moment. All the banter and all the taunting has collided into this single second: when his sinful gaze lifts slowly, and his eyes meet mine, it's all ablaze.

He searches my features. It's a beat of uncertainty, and it occurs to me that he might not have ever intended to touch me. Hesitation catches on his every move as I rethink what led us here. He ordered the others to do his dirty work. He had them tie me and strip me and now . . .

The coward.

"You don't have the balls," I realize with a sneer.

His eyebrows lift high.

"You'll regret saying that," he whispers between us on a warm breath.

My smile slices harder. "Promises, promises," I coo to him.

Big hands slide down my curves, and a shiver races after them. His calloused touch is like fire blazing over my hips, ass, thighs. And then he's kneeling at my feet. I feel like a goddess. I brought him to his knees with ease.

In the end, he'll be the one filled with regret. Even if I can't seem to reach the dark magic inside myself, I've already loosened my bindings enough to form a plan.

His mouth is just a hot breath away from the lace of my panties. Dark, devious eyes peer up at me, blocking out any other person or sound or thing. For a tension-held moment, it's only me and this mysterious Carnal. He's as captivating as the faint magic that lives inside of me. His gaze is as lost as that magic too.

And he's all I think about as his lips part, and his mouth covers my sex from over the thinnest layer of black lace. Heat explodes across my sensitive skin, and the press of his tongue rolling over my mound is enough to tear the gasp from my throat and steal away all of my air as well as my thoughts.

What are you doing!? My logical, exasperated mind yells.

But I don't hear it.

Waves of sensuous tingling glides through my core, my very soul. It's a consuming command like he himself could make me cum with a single press of his dirty mouth against my body.

I've never felt like this. I've never been so lost in the touch of a man.

The moan that shakes over my lips is uncontrollable. But it does cause realization to strike. My eyes flash open wide, and a wicked smile curves his lips as he laps over my clit once more.

A shudder of a breath slips out, but I have to remember the objective here. Even if he is really, *really* good at distracting me.

My legs shift around him as he works his talented mouth. When my thighs press around his head, he only smiles harder, his lashes closing as if he's enjoying the way he makes me squirm. But I'm focused now . . . entirely . . . fuck, he's good at that . . .

Focus!

My thighs clamp firmer around him. I'm locked in against him. Rough stubble meets my smooth flesh. And then I tighten my legs even more.

Around his neck.

Wide eyes flash open. The firm press of his hands becomes a frantic clawing. He can't breathe. My thighs tighten. His sputtering gasp is warm across my damp pussy. Those dark, chaotic eyes are no longer sultry but vengeful.

He isn't afraid. He's furious.

And I know, when he wakes, he'll want me dead.

Just one more name to add to my list of who to watch my back around in this vicious kingdom.

But it's him or me.

And it's not going to be me.

With one more quick press of tension, his lashes flutter. And then I part my legs and let him drop with a heavy thud. My feet fling up, and my ankles catch me on the highest part of the pole. My fists flex, and my arms break the bindings holding me hostage at my new spider-like position.

I crawl backward to put more space between me and the dozens of surprised onlookers.

"If that one's your leader," I shout to them over murmuring voices, "you should really look into getting a more competent leader of hazing. If its leader of orgasms you're looking for, then yes, I agree, he is definitely your guy. But very poor hazing skills. Two out of ten. I've had better." A few of them look up at me with angry scowls, but for the most part, confusion seems to be their emotion of choice.

I just don't care. Especially as I fling myself out into the cool night air, leap away from the carousel, and stride quickly from their little party.

Their leader will find me again when he comes to. I'll be ready . . . As soon as I find my pants.

But more importantly, I'll never let him lay a hand on my little sister.

No man ever will.

I'll protect her.

I'll protect her the way I wish someone would have protected me.

Unless I die trying . . .

CHAPTER SEVEN

Synder

Bellatrix Cuore is a dead woman walking.

The sun rose on my hungover face, and I found myself alone on a spinning ride from the most depraved part of hell. But unlike some of my trysts, I remember last night. *Vividly.* And I've spent the last six hours since then digging into a rather mundane past for a woman who likes to suffocate men with her thick thighs and devious lies.

And what did I find out about this mystery girl?

She's basically a fucking human.

My jaw clenches hard just thinking about what I let her do to me in front of the others. I let my guard down. She distracted me.

And it won't happen again. Especially after finding that other kingdoms have an interest in her as well.

A human girl. The Fae are suspicious of the human

girl. Which makes her monotonous existence very, very interesting.

A heavy, black cloud hangs over the afternoon crowd as I stare a hole through her shiny, black locks and straight through her twisted little mind. Sharp, catlike green eyes look back at me. An amused pissed-off smile tilts her cherry lips, and a line of fucking fire blazes between our gazes.

But she turns away like I'm nothing.

"Ahhhooohhh, your supernatural dick is so hard for Miss Thigh Master, huh, Syn." Benton's laughter shakes through him and across every nerve I possess as I think about the irony of that little nickname.

"Not exactly," I tell my little brother.

"Think she'll take King Leavon's bait?"

I consider the speech that I know is about to ring out over this crowd of newcomers. It's the same one year after year. The King is wise to present it to them while their rational minds can think it over.

But he knows well enough to set the deadline at midnight. When all rationality goes out the hellacious window.

"She's smarter than that." I know she is. She might be a bitch, but she's a clever bitch. She won't sign her life away to a man like Leavon.

Even if he is just as much of a clever bitch.

"Good afternoon, Newcomers," Leavon's smooth, confident voice greets the crowd like a god come to life. Come to save us all.

Or sacrifice us many.

I've been a part of the Brotherhood for a few years. Just long enough to hate the man I'm supposed to consider a brother. But I have a brother. The only family that I've got, but it's enough to know family doesn't use you. And Leavon, he uses everyone.

"I do hope my home of like-minded Carnals have shown you that there is a place for those who do not belong. The others—the Pure, as they'd like to call themselves, they may not understand us, they may cast us out, but we are not animals. We are not the beasts the High Fae like to refer to us as. We're not the sign of times as the mortals may claim. We're beings just like them. Our hearts all beat the same. People like to throw stones at those they do not understand." His tone grows generically gentle, and the crowd of Carnals eat that shit up. The newcomers, the humans especially, nod at his last line of remorse.

No one likes a Monster. And no one likes to feel like a Monster.

And Leavon sells that fact hard.

These people will buy it all up in droves.

Except her.

My arms fold, and I leave my brother's side as I stride quietly through the crowd like the beast I know I am. I don't sugarcoat it like my Brotherhood. I'm a monstrous fuck in my natural form. The magic of the darkness makes my life easier. It aids me in an appearance of normal. Beautiful even. Over the last few years, my magic has blossomed in this shithole.

That's how I know I'll never leave.

And it isn't because of our king's pretty words.

I glance at him high on his golden balcony once more, and the wind sweeps away particles of his flesh in the breeze. From this distance, his features are hard to make out, but the sand will always show.

The people I pass instinctively step aside while others aren't nearly as Carnal as their heritage might allow them to think. My shoulder hits theirs steadily, and I hear a few murmurs as I brush on by them one by one. When I'm just behind her, shadowing over her slender frame, her posture tightens. Her shoulders straighten like she might assassin kick right off the ground and smother me with her sweet thighs once more: a death many men have dreamed of, but only few know the reality.

It's fucking bullshit is what that reality is!

But she's one of the good ones, more Carnal than her human heritage might seem. She's an equal to myself. I can tell by the way she senses me without even seeing me. Evil knows evil.

Villainous, pussy-suffocating bitch!

"Can I help you?" she asks flatly, never once taking her eyes off of something in the crowd.

I clear my throat to reply, but she rudely cuts me off once more.

"Perhaps you're confused. I've read that concussions like you suffered often cause confusion."

My gaze narrows on her shiny black hair once more.

Fucking claustrophobia-inducing cunt!

"It's not a concussion, actually," I tell her as smoothly as the man speaking out to the crowd. "I just had some terribly bad pussy last night. So bad it put me right to sleep halfway through."

The chuckling laughter from behind me tells me that Benton has followed me. He always does.

At the moment, I appreciate it.

My soaring confidence falls slightly when she nods in agreement.

"I know what you mean." She tilts her head to look at me, her illuminating green eyes catching the sunlight through the thick clouds. "Have you ever had head so bad, you'd rather kill the person than tell them they're nowhere near your clitoris?"

A booming chuckle so loud that the people around us start to glance our way causes me to regret the man I call a brother. I toss him a grimace from over my shoulder, and his laughter shudders out into a coughing fit.

Yeah. Choke on your amusement, traitor.

"Meet me here tonight. At midnight," the king tells the crowd. "Choose to join my court." I scoff at the word *court*. He's a king by his own crowning but don't ever say that to his face if you're keen on the heart beating in your chest. Not all of us have forgotten the prosperous Dragon King. "Be welcomed by your own kind and find a life you deserve in the beautiful Kingdom of Carnal."

Clapping and cheering erupt all around, and it's then, among the distraction, that I strike.

My fist snatches through that soft, thick hair right at the root. Her head angles back, exposing the pretty length of her throat, but she doesn't react. She doesn't cause a scene or attract attention to the two of us. My chest melds against her back as I hold her as close to me as I possibly can to drive this point home.

"Do not ever disrespect me again, Bellatrix Cuore. If our paths cross again, I won't hesitate to kill you." Her scent washes over me and my eyes close for just a short moment to take her in.

From above her tall frame, I spy the pull of her lips carving up in a smile that doesn't at all seem threatened

She's either still crazy in the daylight, or she's very, very good at faking her calmness.

Her hand drops fast, and before I can react, her nails are digging through my pants and twisting. *Hard.* Around my fucking balls.

My groan is a silenced sound against her throat as I tense around her, never once releasing my hold on her. Never once feeling her hold lessen on me. The pain that strikes thorugh me sadly shows her a side of me I'd like to keep very far away from an enemy like her.

Because as she hurts me, my cock only grows harder for more.

She ignores it. She's so damn good at ignoring the growl that's turning to a groan along the soft curve of her neck.

"Be careful who you threaten, Synder Steel. Your king cannot always protect you. Even among the Brotherhood."

She releases me and takes a confident step, putting a fair amount of distance between us.

But I don't let her walk away.

I jerk her back by her silken hair, and the redheaded woman at our side is watching us closely. So closely, I give her a sultry wink before pressing my lips like a caress against my lover's throat.

Or so it seems.

The razor blade between my teeth is flicked out fast and sharp, and I nick her flesh just lightly, just enough to tell her I could have slit her throat to the bone. I *could have* killed her in a heap of her pretty, crimson blood if she'd been any more of a pain in my fucking ass.

But I didn't.

An intake of a sharp breath is her reply, and it brings a pleased smile to my lips from around the dripping blood of the blade. My tongue slips out to taste the warmth.

I drop the razor blade from my lips, and it falls back

into my palm as quick as it came before I slide it into my leather belt where it belongs.

Her delicious gasp still rings in my mind as I hiss intimately against her ear. "*Do not* fuck with me, Bella."

And then I shove her away. Her hand slips over her throat, but she doesn't look back at me as I storm off through the crowd of applauding newcomers.

Benton rushes after me, and I see him hand her a jacket for warmth before following after me.

I roll my eyes and ignore his kindness. Someday, he'll learn that even your kindness has a price to pay.

With a crack of thunder, the rain pours down, soaking over me like the realization that sinks in: Bellatrix Cuore knows my place in this kingdom. She knows I'm of the Brotherhood. Just like me, she's done her research.

Which is exactly what King Leavon teaches his Chosen brides in their classes.

My name is on her hit list now.

Just like hers is on mine.

CHAPTER EIGHT

Bella

The splatters dropping down from the sky turn to a drizzle and then to a full downpour by nightfall. Despite my feminine urge to find Synder Steel and put that pathetic little razor blade to good use, I hurry into the city and find a familiar tradesman. The witch doctor doesn't recognize me, but I'd know his violet eyes anywhere.

The white umbrella above him shields him and him alone from the rain. I stand soaking in the cold, but it'll be worth it. His small cart is cluttered with veils. Some are for mutations, some for shapeshifting corrections, some are as simple as an herbal birth control.

But I know exactly what I need.

What my chaotic mind needs.

"Do you have any Reality Rippers?"

His lips twitch at the slang name of the drug I've long forgotten the correct term for.

He nods and lifts a jar from the cart with ten little white pills inside.

I hate pills.

But I hate losing my mind every night too. One of these a night and I'll be sane . . . or as sane as I normally am, anyway.

"I'll give you ten strands of virgin's hair for it."

Not mine, of course. My sexy slut bus left the station a long, long time ago. But I did snatch a few strands off of the sweet boy's coat after he and Synder left. He really should be careful being so kind to strangers like that.

The witch doctor's lavender brows lift high, but as normal, he says nothing.

He offers up the jar, and I sprinkle the short brown hairs into his palm. Rain splatters our hands before I can nod to him with appreciation and rush my ass back through the rain to find Ivy.

The dry pill slides over my tongue and down my throat as the crowd gathers below the balcony once more. I scan each face through the thick rain and finally find her. Three other girls linger at her side. Something strange blooms in my chest as I watch the girls snicker behind their hands as they walk and talk like they've been friends for all their short, shiny lives.

How does she do that? How does Ivy lure people in without even trying?

A tall figure blocks out the little light that the crimson will-o'-wisps provide. I don't focus on him much until he comes closer in through the sheet of rain. He walks my way, and my gaze is set intently on him.

Ruiner's bright eyes are the first thing I notice. My heart leaps to find him again. He doesn't once meet my gaze though.

He brushes past me, ignoring me intently.

When we're side by side, he slows his gait.

"I have to stay for a while. I can't leave. I'll get you out of here, but it'll take some time."

"Oh—"

"Don't speak to me. Don't seek me out."

He buttons his black cloak with patience before looking up, past me. I don't know why it hurts my chest to watch him ignore me. It must be for our protection, but my heart doesn't seem to understand that rationality.

I focus my gaze away from the enormous man at my side. I nod once. Still he doesn't look at me.

My heart drums for his attention across my face or his voice against my name, but I try not to let it get to me. Stop being irrational, Bellatrix.

He takes another step past me, but at the last minute, his fingers brush mine. It's a slick, fleeting touch, but I feel it everywhere.

Slowly my eyes close, and a soft smile pulls at my lips.

Yeah. I'm still fucking crazy even with the pills.

Without another word, he's gone.

My wet hair hangs heavily around my face while I stand in Leavon's courtyard. The divots in the dirt are heaping puddles that send memories sloshing through my mind. Memories of fights in the rain and dark magic that slaughtered more than it should have. Especially between friends.

My eyes close at the thought of who I used to be once upon a time in this courtyard.

When they open, I'm looking up at our king.

The cold seeps in through my clothes even with the kid's jacket wrapped tightly around myself. The constant rain of this kingdom is too much to stand here and listen to Leavon blab on for an hour.

My teeth grind as I stare up at the balcony through the sheet of rain. I can't see him, but I'll always sense him. It's a sensation of wanting to burn bridges and never cross them ever again.

It's what I intended to do.

And yet, here I stand once again as his pupil and courtier.

His Chosen.

"Ah, you've made the right choice, my friends," Leavon calls out, his voice booming through the storm with strange magic.

"He's so dramatic," I hiss to myself.

"You should hear him during a festival," a man at my side chimes in . . .

As if I asked him.

Manic laughter and deadly commands flash within my mind of a festival long gone. But one I'll remember for the rest of my life.

"I hope I never get the pleasure."

The humming laughter is a gentle soothing sound, and I can't pretend not to be interested enough to ignore the stranger at my side. My hair tilts back just slightly, but when I glance out of the corner of my eye, he too is peering at me from behind rain-soaked, black hair. Black eyes study the long length of my frame. But his eyes meet mine all the same.

And a slow, carving smile curves his full lips so far back, I just know he literally eats people for a living.

Nope.

Stop ya right there. Those ones are the deadliest. My logical mind springs to life like a cock-blocking assassin.

Dammit.

I peer up toward Ivy once more. Her head is tilted back, and she's silent as she listens intently to Leavon.

"So please, over the next week, my home is your home." *My destiny is yours,* I think like an echo as he starts his next recited line. "My destiny is yours. Welcome." The sound of heavy gears and barred walls parting is heard through the pounding rain. The group ahead of me, my sister included, stride toward the gates that are now open somewhere up ahead, and I have to be on my way if I'm going to protect her.

I walk away from the crowd.

Until I disappear entirely.

I CLIMB THE WINDOWSILLS WITH QUICK HAND placements and kicking boots until I'm at the third floor. I trained for this. When I was here, I was urged to build my strength and my magic.

And when I left, I never stopped building those things. Except it wasn't to impress Leavon anymore. It was to protect myself from him.

The Chosen rooms were on the third floor when I was here. Let's hope they still are.

My slick footing barely heaves me over the window's ledge, and I can hear the laughter of the crowd rising from the floors below.

The others will be here in minutes.

I scurry down the corridor. In the candlelight, I scan the nameplates of the new occupants on the doors. The letters are a blur to me until I spot the one circling my mind over and over.

Ivy Cuore.

And below her name is another. I was prepared for that. Every Chosen has a Carnal roommate who helps them adjust and advises them.

I can be that person.

I slip Bethory Hallins little name off the door, and the clank of it clattering down the corridor is a nerve-racking sound, but it's done.

A sigh of contentment eases from my lungs at how easy it was to become her roommate.

I push open our door, and . . . fuck.

"You must be Ivy!" A bubbly little demon whore beams at me with a toothy, white smile.

I blink at her for several seconds.

"Bethory?" I ask with a slow, churning smile of my own.

Her head rattles a happy yes.

"An important-looking woman with a clipboard downstairs was just asking for you actually." I point my thumb over my shoulder.

Bethory's smile turns serious.

That's what clipboards do. They're very serious, you know.

"Oh. Okay." She rattles her bright, blonde head a bit more but ultimately scuttles urgently past me, out the door down the hall, and . . .

She fucks right off.

Perfect.

I chuck the satchel of hers off of my bed and let it tumble through the third story window before closing out the cold night air. I have mere seconds to take a seat on the small bed before the door opens slowly once more.

And I'm ready.

Ivy's shining eyes are black as night, something I've never seen at home. Her big gaze meets mine for the first time in . . . *forever*. I was expecting us to be home by now. I was prepared to do whatever it took to keep her safe.

I wasn't prepared for her to forget me.

The twisting sickness of that thought churns through my stomach, but I smile charmingly anyway.

"Ivy?" I stand with my own offering of pleasantries though I'm not as good at it as Bethory, but my sister seems excited to see me, nonetheless.

"I've never stayed away from home before," she says with a confidence only dark magic can bring. It's foreign to me, and my smile falters only slightly before I pull it back up into place.

"We'll have the best of times." And I mean it. I believe it. What little time we share here, it'll be friendship and trust built up all over again.

We don't need Pete Davidson's sexy smile to form a friendship between us. We just need each other.

. . . I hope.

"What's your heritage? Demon Descent? Shadow Demon? Horny Devil? Soul Eater? Imp?" She rattles off more and more, but I've already bitten back my tongue.

The Kingdom of Carnal homes a lot of demons, it's true. But also outcasts of all sorts. Leavon finds what each girl is good at, and he has them focus on that until the magic here really brings it to life. Anyone can be a simple demon in this world. But some, some are Jackals, Zombies, and Skinwalkers. The Kingdom of Carnal accepts them all.

Even the freaks like me.

I can't tell her what my true background is. Because

if I reveal too much, it might link us too closely. That can cause distrust. And I don't want her untrusting of me. I want her trust, and I want her to come home with me. Willingly.

It's the only way.

"Succubus," I say lamely. God, the sex demons are the worst. Get a real power and grow up already.

"Oh," she says wide-eyed and innocently.

A hard smile curves my lips at her understanding of my "magic." She's the same sweet little girl who would beg me hunt fireflies with her and hide beneath the bed from Mom.

"Is it . . . is it wild?"

"The wildest," I tell her with a sultry smile.

I may not truly be a horny, sex-addicted Monster, but I'm a woman all the same. And yeah, sex, it's nice. It's the empty small talk and lies guys give me after that ruins it.

Her giggle is a symphony of memories in my mind that warms me all throughout.

Until a bursting sound bangs through the small bedroom.

And there stands Bethory. Drenched from the rain like a wet dog.

"You lied!" An accusatory finger flings my way, and I stare back at the woman as if I've never seen her a day in my life. Certainly not today, anyway.

"I'm sorry, who are you?" I lift a delicate hand to

my chest as if I've been fatally wounded by her accusation.

Her jaw nearly detaches and hits the floor with how wide-mouthed she's gaping right now.

"You know who I am! You threw me out and tossed my panties to the wind!" She holds up a wad of fabrics.

Panties.

Hmm. I knew her satchel seemed light, but I assumed it was more than just underwear . . .

I pause just long enough for someone else to step in: my sweet sister.

"Listen, I don't know who you are, but you need to take your," her big eyes glance to the panties, "take your stuff and go find your own room. This is a privately assigned room selected by King Leavon himself."

My brows lower fast. The king personally selected Ivy. *That* is not good. Not good at all.

"This is my room!" the lunatic shouts at us, angry fists shaking around a rainbow of muddy under-garments.

Ivy's palms plant on her hips, and I'm actually impressed with the confidence this place has given her. I've never seen her like this.

"Is there a problem in here?" a smooth voice like violence wrapped in velvet asks tensely.

"Yes!" Bethory booms as she spins on her heels.

And comes face-to-face with Synder Steel.

Why? Why is this man always two steps away from crawling up my ass and setting up a nice little bed-and-breakfast for himself to stay in for the rest of our miserable lives?

"This is my room. They're forcing me out of *my* room!"

"This is Ivy's room. Her name's on the door, personally selected by the king." Synder glances my way from over pale, disheveled blonde hair but draws his attention back when a hard stomping of Bethory's foot meets the floorboards.

"Ahhh! It's my fucking room! She lied, and she's lying right now, and that's my bed, and my new best friend, and this is mine, and I'm not leaving!"

A big hand clasps over Bethory's face. He snatches up her entire face and forces her to look at him. Synder stares down on her with unblinking, starry eyes. "Listen to me, girl. As the Brotherhood, I'm commanding you to vacate not only this room but the Kingdom of Carnal. You were ill selected. A mistake. And I won't tolerate your screaming for another bloody second." His mouth twitches oddly, morphing almost, but it seems to halt when his teeth grind tightly together.

I watch in awe of his power as the protests from Ivy's previous roommate halt entirely. She nods her head emptily. The girl steps back robotically. She doesn't make a sound. She doesn't look our way at all. And then she walks right out the door.

Damn. I should have handled all of this like that.

A boy, much younger than Synder, steps into the doorway and peers around. It's the boy who gave me his coat. His eyes are snake-like, an intense green that no human could ever possess. He glides in that way too. His gait feels slithering with a swaying carefulness to his every step.

"Thank you," Ivy says quietly, looking to Synder with kindness I don't like one bit.

"You're lucky," the boy behind Synder cuts in, drawing Ivy's attention to him in an instant. The split of his tongue catches against his words, but his tone is soft. Kind. "You're lucky you're neighbors with a future Brotherhood like me."

Synder rolls his eyes so hard, I swear he's mentally placing a curse on the kid. Meanwhile, Ivy's soft laughter is an alluring sound, it seems. Because the boy steps past Synder and offers her his hand.

"Benton Steel," the young boy says with bedroom eyes focused intently on my little sister.

I make note of his interest, a double underlined note to look into his name and background.

Honestly, his attention is better than Synder's, and that's all that matters in this moment. He's her age. Which doesn't make him any less dangerous, but it does make me feel better for some reason.

"You're his mentor?" I ask with a smirk clinging to my lips. "They really do have to stop putting you in leadership roles, Syn." Synder's galaxy-like eyes flash with lightening, and the image of his mouth kissing down my sex is fresh in my mind. Only Benton seems to find my joke amusing.

Synder's lip curls hard, but he holds my gaze.

"You didn't tell me Her Thighness was so funny." Benton sends his elbow in to meet Synder's ribs, and the literal jab only pisses him off even more.

Her Thighness. I like it. I shall reign over men for all of time. Long Live her Thighness.

"Right. Benton will be next door to the left. Try not to attract any more psychopaths," Synder advises as if he himself isn't a total fucking psychopath.

But I don't get a chance to say that. Because he turns abruptly around and leaves. His brother passes Ivy a long and flirtatious look as he backs away.

"There are two of us here on the Chosen's floor. Consider me your protector though. I'll walk you to your Carnal Class in the morning. I'm here if you ever need me to take care of any more psychos," he tells her with a charming smile.

The door clicks closed with a resounding sound of quiet.

"Thank god I didn't really get a crazy bitch like her for a roommate." Ivy laughs and laughs as I force a frozen smile to my lips like broken glass gleaming back at her.

And try not to let my crazy show.

CHAPTER NINE

Bella

She sleeps soundly. She sleeps like a girl who hasn't yet been hurt by the world. And that's exactly why I'm lacing up my boots without a sound by our bedroom door.

What does the king want with a girl like Ivy? She's sweet. Kind. Everyone loves her. He has to know she's too young to be his Chosen.

But decades have passed. And this kingdom is still as poor as the day I first stepped foot here.

He's desperate. Even his classes seem hurried. If I remember right, we had a party that lasted three days when I was a Chosen. These girls are being rushed into classes after one day.

But he needs to fuck right off and stop giving her *special* attention. God, why did he have to pick her?

A memory rings around my mind with a sharp pain that splinters through me every time I think of it.

"You're special to me, Trix. No one's shown you your worth, but I promise, I will."

Long fingers push back the hair brushing my cheek. I don't have a clue what to say to someone so wise and charming. My ex hated when I ruined a moment like this. So I say nothing. A shy smile tenses my lips as I hold his adamant gaze.

The way he looks at me, no one has ever looked at me like this. His golden eyes shine like a man who has spent his entire life searching for a long-lost treasure. And I'm it.

The Sand Man's rough, lithe body covers mine, and emotions like I've never felt wallow within my chest as he presses down on me. Confusion. Love. Sadness. It all swirls into one.

It consumes me.

Then he consumes me.

I blink away the sickening memories, but my gaze can't pull away from the way the pale moonlight highlights her sharp angelic face. She's grown, but she still looks like that little girl who used to beg me to read *Brown Bear, Brown Bear* before bed. Her giggles as I'd twist the repetitive lines into animal voices and joking puns dance through my thoughts.

He's going to wreck her.

Unless I stop him.

My palm presses the door closed without a sound,

and I'm a shadow in the halls as I tread down to the first floor. And keep going to the lowest part of the castle.

King Leavon's chambers.

Some would call it a dungeon. I would. I'd definitely call it a fucking torture chamber. But as for our king, he simply calls it a bedroom. The dungeon halls aren't drafty and chilling, despite my nerves that are crawling to get out. Every thought in my head is urging me to turn around, run away from this sinister land, and never come back again.

Especially after what I did to Melissa.

My lashes close hard with a wincing memory, but I shake it off and press myself close to the wall as I creep up to the solitary door at the end of the corridor. That's what it is though. Everything is just memories upon memories that suffocate my mind. The meds my mother gave me, they helped. But I'd rather remember the dark parts than forget who I am.

White light floods out into the heavy darkness from the crack of the partially open door. A smooth and calming voice calls out through the opening, and the blood in my face drains cold the moment I hear him speak.

"What kind of disturbance?" Leavon asks.

The light hits my eye, and I spy him lounging carelessly on the end of his large spanning bed. Tight black pants hang low on his hips while hard line clatter up a chest I've touched too many times to feel anything but disgust when I look at the beautiful man.

"A girl on the third floor was causing problems for Ivy."

Shit. I know that voice.

"Did you take care of her, Synder?" the king's concern is so deep in his tone that it nearly sounds endearing.

If you didn't know him.

"She won't be coming back," Synder confirms.

"Who . . . Who did we assign as her roommate? Anyone that can help look after her?"

Shit. Shit. Shit.

If he says my name, it's over. Leavon will remember me and the year we spent together. He'll remember the way I fled at dawn without so much as a goodbye or fuck you or anything of the sort.

"Bellatrix Cuore."

My heart's beating is paused indefinitely as he says my last name that matches Ivy's.

This is how I die. He's going to kill me. He's going to—

"Huh. Will this Bellatrix be a good protector for Ivy?" The king asks with total fucking disregard for our past relationship.

"That motherfucker," I hiss.

How dare he not have the half a brain to remember the woman whose entire life he ruined? The sixteen-year-old girl who he raped, used, and abused!

But that's the thing. I'm just a number among all

the women he has destroyed. I'm just a second on a clock, passing by, never to be thought of again.

Once more, though, I hang on unspoken words. I know Synder has looked into me. Does he know I was here just years ago? Will he tell his Brotherhood of his suspicions?

"She seems dense but capable."

"What the fuck!" I hiss once more.

"Good. Good." The king nods his empty little head, and I'm seething to slam my fist into his perfect nose and perfect teeth. "Bring her to me."

My mouth falls open, and my boots stumble over themselves in the darkness. My stealth is a forgotten trait, and my mind reels with only one thought: Get. The. Fuck. Out.

White light crashes over me. It freezes over my face. And I lock eyes with the one man I can't seem to get away from.

Synder's head tilts as he studies me and my red-handedness.

With parted lips, I wait for him to call out to Leavon. I wait for the jig to be up and for my head to be on a chopping block.

Except it never happens.

With a smooth sweep of his hand, he closes the door behind him. A deep darkness falls across us, and I'm tempted to flee right here and now and hope by morning he thinks this bizarre moment was just a hallucination brought on by the gasses down in this fucking dump of a torture chamber.

A hot breath washes over my ear, and his sudden closeness alone sends shivers racing down my arms.

"Do you value your life so little?"

I blink at that and try not to think too much about the way his bare chest brushes against the curve of my breasts. My nipples harden beneath the thin shirt.

"What do you mean?" I ask honestly.

I value my life plenty. I certainly valued it enough to get the hell out of here once before.

"You're always just seconds away from being tossed into a situation that can get you killed." His hand ghosts down the line of my jaw, and the intimacy of it is a clash of confliction. It's a sweet caress. Until his fingers thread through my locks, and he grips me by the back of my neck. "Just like now," he says.

And then I'm thrown through the door and into the light. My palms and knees hit hard on the uneven stones of the cold flooring. Memories of being pressed down against this floor flood my mind, and the tangled moments I spent with Leavon thrusting on top of me rushes vomit to burn across the back of my throat.

I let my dark hair hide my features. Fear of him finding me thrashes through me. The king takes his time to bring his attention to the woman spilled across his bedroom floor. His shining eyes lock with mine, and I know he's about to call me out. The nights we spent together are slamming through his head right now. He's about to murder me for coming back to him after all these years.

"What was your name again?" The jackass asks instead.

Oh. Come the fuck on!

"Bellatrix, My King," I say instead with my head lowering hard to hide the rage in my eyes.

He ruined my fucking life and doesn't even have the kindness to remember my fucking name?! He's going straight to hell. Or where ever Sand Man Monsters like this fucker go when someone inevitably stabs a knife through his little sandpaper heart.

"Bellatrix, you have a roommate, Ivy. She is very important to this kingdom." His bare feet brush over the floor with a lazy, scuffing sound, and the hammering of my heart is all I hear when he hunches down in front of me. Little particles of sand waft through the air as a long finger meets my chin and tips my face up at him. His hand slides into mine, and he lifts me to my feet, never once taking his gaze off of mine.

Pain and hurt sting through me at the simplicity of our closeness. We're face-to-face but too many years and unforgivable sins separate us. It feels crushing. It feels like revulsion.

I fucking hate you! I hate you! I—

"Of course, my Lord," I murmur.

"You're pretty, Bellatrix," he whispers to me, his

hand skimming over the scar that lines my face and brushing down the column of my throat.

How could he forget the scar this fucking kingdom caused?

"Thank you," I grind out with a hint of a smile. I lift my lashes once more and barely spot the look he passes to the man standing behind me.

He looks to the asshole I nearly forgot I loathed because of this new asshole I'm currently trapped in front of. It's a surplus of assholes right now. No one needs this many. One is one too many.

"Are you . . . the curious type, Trix?" And just like that. With the simple use of the nickname he gave me, flashes of agony cut through me. Nights of tears and shame and fear and rage cover my body in a chill of terrible memories I thought I'd forgotten. It all suffocates me.

He raped me! And I had done so damn well to repress every touch he ever gave me.

Until now.

"W—what do you mean, My King?" I ask innocently. Because I know he likes that. He doesn't like smart women. He doesn't like women who ask too many important questions. He likes the ones who trust him fully.

He likes the ones he can use and abuse.

The warmth of his palm is heavy as it lowers down my throat, my collarbone, my breast.

My throat tightens.

"I can sate all of your curiosities, Trix." The heat of his lips just beneath my ear burns water beneath my closed eyes.

I'm strong. I'm not that little girl anymore. I can do this.

I won't give up the ruse. I won't tap out. Because Ivy's life is worth more than mine. And I'll suffer his touch all over again to save her the misery.

Another press of a hand skims over my stomach, and my body reacts hard, my stomach knotting so much, I think I might vomit. When his chest brushes over my back, I meld into him. I sink into Synder's body to flee Leavon's.

And strangely . . . he lets me.

The king turns me like I'm a mop to be dragged across his floors, and I'm face-to-face with the man I've hated for the last two days.

But it doesn't feel like hate in this moment. It feels like salvation.

He sees it in the lock of our eyes. My breath is too fast. It isn't lustful, it's fearful.

And I think Synder sees that.

Leavon's fingers pull at the neck of my cotton shirt. It rips there with ease beneath his strength. His icy hands are like spiders crawling down my back, and all I can think of are the times he used me to forget himself. The nightmares I wanted to keep covered come clawing up through layers and layers of dirt that I've buried them under.

I can't breathe.

Synder's touch turns gentle against my hips. He pulls me close, but it isn't demanding. It's entirely calming.

"Focus on me," he whispers like a prayer against my ear.

My lashes flicker open and then closed, and I nod hard to him. I can't stop nodding. I can't—I can't.

I slam my lips to his. Tension lines his entire body as he holds me loosely and waits. But for what, I don't know. I part his lips with a flick of my tongue, and he takes me in without question. All the shitty things we've said to each other aren't spoken. They aren't thought of at all.

Because he feels good. His fingers press harder to my hips, but he doesn't drag me against him. He doesn't pin me down and fuck me until he's done.

He simply lets me lose myself in him.

The protection of my thin shirt falls low, exposing myself, but it doesn't matter. Because Synder melds into me, covering my nakedness with his smooth, hard chest. But it doesn't stop the cold, crawling fingers from slipping between the heat of our bodies. Big hands cover my nipples, rolling them and teasing them and making me kiss the beautiful man in front of me even harder. I kiss him like I want to fall into him and hide.

Lips brush against my ear, kissing lightly there before the creeping waft of his breath meets my skin once more.

"Give me your word you'll protect Ivy, and I'll give you so, so much, Trix," Leavon promises like a fool who doesn't know I'll protect Ivy with my last dying breath.

But I want nothing from him.

Especially this.

Synder pulls back from me, leaving me gasping against his lips as he stares his starry gaze into my big, pleading eyes.

"She's friends with the girl," Synder says suddenly. Betrayal is a word screaming out to me over and over in my mind. He's going to betray everything he knows about me in this very moment. "I think—I think something like this might cause jealousy or issues between them," Synder explains.

I blink at his expression, but he's ungiving of any emotion. *What is this cruel Monster thinking, and why did he say that?*

Leavon's assault against my breasts halts immediately. He stares blankly over my head like he's lost in thoughts he'll never be able to climb out of.

"Fucking her roommate will cause problems between the two women, My King," Synder explains rather harshly.

Leavon drops my breasts like he doesn't know how they got in his grubby little hands to begin with.

"Leave me," Leavon orders like a true king of commands. He turns his back on me and strides to his bed.

Synder's palms slip away somewhat regretfully, and I can't explain the feelings tangling inside of me.

Thank you, I mouth to him.

As always, his blank expression reveals no hint of his thoughts. He isn't a kind man who does kind things. But for some reason, he protected me from Leavon.

And I'll always remember that.

With my hand covering my torn shirt against my chest, I slip past him. I pull open the door with the means of rushing down the dark corridor and never looking back.

Except I do.

And when I peer back over my shoulder, those starry eyes are watching me.

Until I'm entirely out of sight.

CHAPTER TEN

THE NIGHT IS STILL heavy with darkness lining the bedroom when I slip in. I close the door with a quiet click, but my steps falter when I look at the bed opposite of my own.

The blankets are reared back. The sheets are tossed aside. The bed is empty.

The pounding of my heart falls fast and hard, and I think through everything I know. Where could she have gone?

I fling open the door once more, but the quiet of the hall is all that I hear.

Shit.

My thoughts race, and a thousand things fling through my mind, but ultimately, only one calms me: she isn't with Leavon. She's out causing mischief that only the darkness of this realm can bring. But she's safe. Or as safe as she can be in a realm full of Monsters.

A sigh that feels endless shoves from my lungs while I pull off my shirt and then pull it back on to tie the ripped material at the front. It's not cute, but it covers my boobs, and as far as crop tops go, that's about all you can ask for.

I sink into my bed. It's all I can do to kick off my boots and pull the blankets up my tired body. I can still feel his cold, crawling touch against my skin. It's a shivering thought that I shove away the moment it creeps into my mind.

I roll to my side, hugging my knees to my chest, and try my damnedest to think of absolutely anything else.

Like Synder.

My lashes fly open.

I really let that asshole kiss me. God, what was I thinking?

I was thinking . . . he saved my ass back there.

But why?

The breath in my lungs feels pressing and harsh. I just want to sleep. I don't want to think of Leavon or Synder or even myself.

I just want to sleep. For days.

"Pretty Monster?" a deep voice whispers.

The scream that tears out of me is an embarrassment to Monsters everywhere. How can they even call me one of their own with a shriek like that?

My fingers fist into my palms as I close my eyes and calm my shaking breaths.

"Ruiner!" I accuse, and I know exactly where he is,

even if I can't see the brooding, beautiful man. "Get out from under my bed! It's not a vacation spot, it's a bedroom. And you have to knock on the door like everyone else!"

His rumbling laughter hums through the room and into my own chest.

How does he do that? How does the simple sound of his velvety voice fill me with warmth?

"What were you doing wandering at night? You know it's not safe," he whispers, worry lacing his rasping words.

I know I scolded him just two seconds ago, but . . . I feel safer knowing he's just beneath my bed. I always have. He's my security blanket.

He's my Monster.

"I was looking for my roommate," I say instead of the truth.

"Lies, lies, lies," he singsong whispers. "I've listened to your confessions for years, Pretty Monster. I know what you sound like when you hide things."

When I hide things.

I close my eyes, and twisted words from the past sneak up in my thoughts.

"The Sand Man didn't hurt me."

"I didn't love him at all."

"I almost forgot about the things he made me do."

"I can't remember my last night in the Kingdom of Carnal."

"Melissa who?"

My eyes fly open and ignore the tone that rings out in all of those statements. He reads me better than I read myself, it seems.

"I just couldn't sleep," I add to the lie, and his rumbling laughter eases the line creasing my brows.

"I know," he says.

My arms fold lightly across my stomach, and it's nice to have him just beneath me, both of us talking like eight long years never happened at all.

It's like I'm a girl again, and he's the only person I can trust in the entire world.

"How do you—" I pause to try to describe it just right, "How do you enter beneath my bed anyway? Is it a summons? I guess it can't be because you've surprised me more than once."

His hum of thought is all that parts the darkness.

"I have to be allowed. I can't just crawl around under anyone's dusty bed cubby."

A smirk quirks my lips.

"So they have to want you there?"

"In a way. I have to be invited. Thought of."

"You think I thought of you?"

"I know you did, Pretty Monster," he says so confidently, I have to bite my lip to stop the smile from growing.

Maybe I should take a second dose of Reality Rippers because I am definitely crazy to be flirting with my best friend.

"I have something for you," he adds when I don't immediately reply.

"A gift?" I ask, my brows lifting high at the idea of a present from a monstrous man like Ruiner.

It could be anything: A shiny charm bracelet with finger bones dangling and clanking beautifully. Maybe a heart-shaped box of chocolates with eyeballs neatly placed in each divider. Perhaps a piece of his own silent soul . . .

A hand nudges my arm, and my mouth falls open when the scar burning along his forearm catches my sight. In the glowing black-and-red light of his fire, a little square of something brown sits delicately in the palm of his enormous hand.

He remains hidden beneath the disheveled blanket of my bed. Only his arm protrudes, and . . .

"What is that?" I ask, not taking the gift at all but staring in confusion at something so normal looking. Definitely not eyeballs.

"It's galaxy cake. It's like a brownie. It'll help you relax and sleep. I eat some every day to keep the darkness from turning me into a psychopath."

I don't mention that I've gotten my own fix for the dark magic of this world, and I also don't mention that I wouldn't mind seeing Ruin in all his full psychopathic glory.

The galaxy cake sounds amazing. I wonder if it's better than the pills. If this snack could replace the Reality

Rippers, I'd happily choose cake every day of the week. I wonder where he got it? He was always so sweet with the seer at the edge of town. She'd give him her remedies for his wounds. Why didn't she help him with his scar?

I take the fluffy brown square from his palm as I think about the woman and how kind she was to him. My teeth sink in, and somehow, it's still warm. It practically melts in my mouth with rich flavors of chocolate and just a slight strange spice of something I can't quite place.

"It's good," I murmur around another big bite.

"Mmm," he hums, and it's then that I realize he's chewing too.

We share the dessert together like kids, and the whole time I think of the seer. She was bewitchingly beautiful.

She—

"She liked you," I say as I finish off the last bite.

"What?" A mumbled voice chokes out around a full mouth.

"The seer at the edge of the kingdom. She was sweet to you. And you were oblivious."

"Fawn?"

"The pretty seer with the curvy hips and fuck-me eyes."

His cough sounds violent at that description.

That's what he gets for talking with a mouth full.

"Fawn didn't have f—fuck-me eyes. She's a motherly type. She loved to help."

108

OF SINS AND PSYCHOS

"Help get you into bed, yes."

"She's a hundred and ninety-three years old, Bella!"

My brows lift high at that, and I find it suddenly hard to get them to come back down to their normal sitting position. I blink slowly.

The galaxy cake is kicking in. Its magical herbal remedy is soothing me as we speak. No darkness shall ever pass my fortress of a mind.

I swallow once more before saying, "There's nothing wrong with dating someone . . . a bit older."

"A bit?!"

My lashes lift without speed. Everything, including my thoughts, feel slow and leisurely. Nothing is a bother in this moment. All my worries over the Sand Man, my sister, hell, even my own well-being isn't important.

Rain taps along my window. Lightening accompanies the steady storm. The beat of the drops on my window is all I can hear despite Ruin's endless commentary that I can't seem to focus on.

What's so bad about wanting to fuck Synder Steel anyway? I think for a long, long moment, but I honestly don't remember. Maybe I will fuck him. He's a nice guy. Super good dude, for sure.

I look up, and there, on the ceiling, is a shadow. I look at it long enough to make shapes out of the mass of it. It looks like a hand. Sort of.

Did it just move?

Ruiner carries on about seers and grandmothers and fuck-me eyes and old folks homes. All while I watch this inky spill of a shadow stretch across the length of the ceiling. It travels from the crack at the top of the door . . .

To right above me.

Two red eyes blink back at me among the mass of shadowy nothingness.

"Ruin?" I whisper casually, interrupting his rant about dentures and kissing. "Ruiner?" I ask again a bit louder until he finally shuts up about the beautiful seer who most definitely wanted to fuck him.

"What?!"

"The galaxy cake, does it cause hallucinations?"

A pause drops in.

"No. Not at all."

I tilt my head at the shadow. Just vaguely, I can make out its own face as it tilts its head right back at me. The length of it shifts, sliding toward the far side of the wall, and it watches me as I follow it with narrowed eyes. Like a wave, it drifts back above my bed.

The two of us watch each other with bated breath.

Then, the dark figure starts to melt.

From its center, the mass drips down from the ceiling ever so slowly. It stretches down, and long fingers form at the end of the oil spill. Then it touches my arm, ghosting down my flesh until a gasp rips from my lips.

"Bella?" Ruiner asks.

"*Bella?*" the shadow repeats on a crawling whisper.

Then the figure drops from the ceiling, and a beautiful man lands on top of me.

A scream in my throat catches as a slender hand covers my mouth. His legs straddle me, and he looks down on me with big fiery eyes. Inky tattoos of gold and crimson lick down his arms and up his neck, skimming lightly around his face with symbols I don't understand.

"You can see me?" he asks, his messy black hair falling into his bright eyes as he cocks his head at me once more.

I nod.

"And feel me?" He runs a long finger across my cheek and jaw line, a shiver tracing his touch as I nod once more.

He's hypnotizing. Magnetic.

And then something big and solid slams through the shadow man. Smoke wafts around me where the stranger just was. Ruiner's wings flap chaotically. Books thunder to the floor while glass shatters across the wall. Strong arms slam down on either side of the man, trapping him against the wall. Ruiner's fist pulls back with intent, and a smile parts the shadow man's lips.

With a pop, smoke wafts through the space, lingering where the stranger once was.

I stare around the room, carefully eyeing every shadow as Ruiner flings the desk in the corner on its side, trashing my bedroom even more with his wild rage.

"He's gone!" I urge before my friend's hand clamps around Ivy's bed frame, and he looks frantically beneath it. "He's gone." I sit at the edge of my mattress, wanting to sink into it and never come out.

Ruiner turns abruptly, and in a matter of seconds, he's kneeling before me. One big hand clasps over my cheek, and knowing eyes search my face.

"What was it?" he asks with heavy confusion.

"I don't know. I—I'm fine," I utter, and even my breath sounds labored and uncertain.

"I can tell when you're lying, Pretty Monster." His thumb pushes back and forth along my jawline.

"Who was that?" I ask instead.

His serious features harden as he shakes his head. "I—I didn't see it. It was all darkness. I could only tell that you needed me." He looks over his shoulder once more, and he's just as skittish as I am.

With or without the cake, I'm never going to sleep now.

Someone attacked me. And only I could see it?

"Would you—would you stay with me? For tonight?"

Why did that sound so pathetic? So fragile and fearful like I'm a fair maiden in a regency romance just waiting for the dude to rip his shirt open already.

"Never mind," I say with a wave of my hands. "It's not a big deal. Shadow men. Monsters under my bed.

Inky blobs falling from my ceiling. It's perfectly normal here."

A smirk twitches at the corner of Ruin's lips.

"I already know when you want me, Bella," he rasps so sensually, the sound of his voice travels right into me and shudders through my core.

Why did that sound so dirty?

"Scoot over." He stands, and I don't make a move.

"What?"

"Scoot over. Be a good host and stop making the men you call in the middle of the night sleep on the damn floor."

"Okay, wait a fucking minute. I don't call you in the middle of the night. You're not a booty call. You're a Monster. Let's clarify that right now."

His dark brows lift high as he stares down on me.

"I'm the man you call in the middle of the night when you can't sleep. I'm the one you want even while you dream. Is that clarifying enough for you?"

Shit, it still sounds bad.

I nod anyway.

And then I scoot my ass over and invite the Monster into my bed.

The mattress dips hard, and I'm thrown into him as his enormous body steals every inch of space the little twin bed possesses. I find myself literally lying on his chest, my leg curled over his knee as I cling to him like that damn regency romance maiden once again.

He feels nice though. My head is heavy as I find

the curve of his arm. I fit perfectly against him. His hip shifts against my core and not even the tension of our closeness fully seeps into my foggy mind.

How hard his body is and how addicting his voice always is, isn't a distraction in this moment.

His arms fold behind his head, and my hair falls across his bicep. The heat of his scar is warm near my cheek, but its glow is nice along his features, accentuating the hard edge of his jaw as he tilts his face upward. In the crimson glow, he looks like a dangerous man. Then his dark lashes close softly, and he looks alarmingly angelic. I can't explain why he looks more like an angel than a terrifying creature.

In a way, he always has been. He has always been my armor in a world full of knives.

He's my protector.

He's my Monster.

CHAPTER ELEVEN

The top floor of Leavon's glorious castle is an old dusty section of the beautiful estate that no one seems to journey into often. I loved it in here.

It's where I met Melissa.

I shake the sinking thought of her from my mind as I shove open the door and let the squeal of the hinges shriek through the empty room. Bright morning sunlight casts in across glittering dust particles in the air.

Four tables with heavy wooden legs sit in formation at the front. At the back are dozens and dozens of bookcases. The tops of them are so high up, I couldn't read the titles there if I tried. A smile tenses my lips.

It's my favorite place in this entire wicked kingdom. *The grand library.*

Brittle pages meet my fingertips as I leaf through the sign-in sheet at the door.

My own name is at the bottom; the very last person to sign in was me. Eight long years ago.

I can only imagine that once upon a time, a ruler far wiser than Leavon had this beautiful room built and glorified.

And now Leavon's letting it rot.

My lips curl at the thought, but I venture down the first aisle of bookcases. I have an hour before Ivy is finished with her morning Carnal Class. All Chosen women have three days of welcoming classes that explain the lay of the land and the magic that settles under your skin with time. With her gaining Leavon's special attention, she'll have more than three days of classes though. She'll go through physical training and mental manipulation for months. He'll put her against other girls, some of them her very best friends, and then he'll see if she's strong enough to be his mate. He'll see if she's the one everyone claims will bring this kingdom endless power.

My teeth are grinding just thinking about it, but I try my best to focus on the creepy shadow issue at hand this morning.

What the hell was that man last night? I'm about to find out.

Two shelves are on either side of me. Small golden plates are along every endcap. When I turn to the one on my left, I lift my finger and slide it across the dusty plate.

The Mayhem of Venereal Diseases

"Huh. Interesting," I say with a nod.

I hum in thought, and though the idea of pages and pages of monstrous venereal cocks does sound fascinating, I turn to the right and run my thumb over that bookcase's plate instead. I rub at the smooth metal, and it gleams like new when I'm done.

Encyclopedias of Realms

"No, thank you. One asinine realm at a time is more than enough for me."

I swipe across a few more plates, walking slowly through the depths of the eerily quiet library. Until finally, two shelves from the back, it seems like what I'm looking for.

The Most Monstrous Beasts of Carnal

"Perfect," I whisper to myself.

I don't know *who* the shadow man was in my room last night, but I might be able to find out *what* he was and where he comes from. And then it'll be me who's stalking up on him among the shadows.

The rows and rows of titles are all so strange, I'm not sure where to begin. I scan a few faded spines of books:

Headless Horses and Men, Bewitching Beauties, Panty Creatures . . .

I suppose it's safe to say the shadow man from last night is none of those. But I didn't see if he rode in on a headless horse either . . . wait, what the hell are Panty Creatures? My thighs shift nervously, and I vow to never glance inside the pages of that bizarre book to ensure I don't give myself a newfound fear of pussy monsters.

A large softbound book just a few rows above my head catches my eye:

Things that Go Bump in the Night

Seems vague.

And accurate.

Dammit. Where are the books titled *Inky Shadow Drips that Create Sexy Monster Men in Your Sleep?*

This will do, I suppose.

I step onto the bottom of the bookshelf for an extra inch of height, and with my arm wrenched high above my head, I flail aimlessly for the book in question. The colossal shelf doesn't sway, but I still feel like a middle schooler about to get detention for climbing around on sacred Ikea shelving. It takes two fumbling tries, but the softbound book wiggles out of its spot with an embarrassing amount of effort and a whole lot of sweat on my brow. With a huff, I blow the hair from my face and flip open the first page before I've even found a seat at the front table.

Images of faceless creatures, Skinwalkers pictured in eerie, slender limbs, and pages and pages of Incubi fill my time for the next half an hour. Seriously, what is with people's obsessive fear of sex demons? *Oh no, the big scary man might give me multiple orgasms and then leave before morning without being asked. Whatever shall I do?*

Probably sleep incredibly peacefully, that's what.

All is silent, and I'm consciously thinking about how little time I have left before meeting Ivy after her morning classes. I have fifteen minutes at best. Twenty if I haul ass down to the first floor fast enough.

Either way, twenty minutes isn't enough to get through this book . . .

A light wind catches my hair as I read. A heavy silence fills my ears. I'm very much aware of the room suddenly. And there's a chill that has settled without a single crack of a window. My lashes lift from the extremely detailed picture of the Incubus cock spanning not one but two full pages.

Seems exaggerated but whatever.

A shadow crawls from one corner of the table to the other, stopping just half an inch from the edge of my open book. I notice it instantly. The hairs on the backs of my arms lift one by one. Still, I don't react. I don't look up. I keep my head down.

And wait.

Because my shadow man isn't a thing that goes bump in the night. He's very much alive and well in the morning sunlight too.

A spot of ink is his first move. It drips down from high above me and splatters at the tip of the elaborate drawing thrusting from page to page. The ink droplet is a rather nice touch if I do say so myself.

The moment a strand of my dark locks lifts, I know his curiosity has gone too far.

And I fling my hand back and grip a fistful of soft hair. My chair tips back on two precarious legs. I'm suspended in time for only a moment. Before we both go crashing down. Wood breaks beneath me, and for a moment, a single fleeting moment, those red eyes are looking down on me.

Until I flip him. And then he's looking up at me. I drag him off the floor by his tight black shirt that wrinkles in my fists, and I slam him into the tabletop.

A slow smile stretches across his hauntingly beautiful face. His gaze lingers on the birthmark that splatters across my chest and kisses my neck. Calculating eyes sweep up over my features, and it's then that I notice the dark shadow fading out of his appearance. Only the golden lines of his elaborate tattoos remain. He's just a man. A very, very handsome, very manic-looking man.

But a man all the same.

"What do you want?" I press into him, and he

simply leans into the surface of the table like it's a luxurious bed.

"I just wanted to say the picture is a bit exaggerated by three—" He glances at the throbbing picture in the book out of the corner of his crimson eyes, "to five inches at least." He speaks like he has a great knowledge of Incubus cocks. He's making a casual mockery of the book as if it has bothered him for years, and he has just now gotten a chance to discuss it with his favorite book club member: me.

"Why are you following me?" I ask more sternly, tempted to slam his back harder into the table just to get his wandering attention back on the issue at hand.

His aloof gaze finds mine once more.

"Why is it you can see me?"

My lip curls as my brows pull together hard. The lashing words on the tip of my tongue falter.

"What!?"

This in-depth conversation feels strange with me pinning him down and him just lying there like it's an afternoon nap. I fling myself off of him and start pacing the library floor. With his elbows, he lifts himself up into a leaning position but stays mostly undisturbed by our little feud.

It's like he isn't even aware of any negativity in life whatsoever.

"Most people, especially humans, they can't see me. Sometimes with enough rising emotion, I can be seen.

Empaths and people with combustible emotions, they can see me. Sometimes with enough force, I can move things, and that gets their attention, but they make excuses for it. Humans like to make excuses. Makes them feel safe."

I'm seeing things that aren't there?

No, he's there. Ruiner saw him too . . .

No, Ruiner protected me from something he couldn't see.

Shit.

"Other Monsters, can they see you?"

His drifting attention finds a squirrel outside the high window, and he seems entranced by the tiny creature and not at all concerned about his actual life.

"Excuse me?!" I blink at him, my arms folding over my chest hard before his eyes come back to find the dullest thing in this room filled with enthralling things.

Me? I'm really that much of a bore?

"You're excused," he offers, confusion pinching his inky brows.

Goddammit! What is with the Monsters in this chaotic realm? Can we just be fucking sane for one minute?!

"Why are you following me?" I bite out.

"Because King Leavon ordered me to."

Finally! Finally, a real answer.

And not a good one.

"The king is having me followed? You're stalking me?" He glances to me, his gaze lingering on the unique birthmark once again, but he doesn't comment.

"Yes. Says you're suspicious, but he can't quite put his finger on it."

I nod solemnly and try not to give too much away.

"And what have you told him about me?"

"That you're rather boring if I do say so myself."

"Boring!" Why am I complaining? He could have told my one enemy that I am indeed a person to be suspicious of, and I'm complaining about being unexciting in this man's eyes?

"You lay in bed last night and ate pot brownies. Alone. Or at least, I thought you were alone."

"They weren't pot brownies!" Wow, I have got to focus on the real issues at hand here. "They were galaxy cakes. To help me sleep."

He arches a dark brow at me so high, it nearly leaps right off his perfectly angular face.

"Galaxy cake? Does that sound . . . does that sound a little like space cake to you?"

My lips part, and before a word of my argument falls out, I close my gaping mouth and realize this shadow man might be onto something.

They did have an awful aftertaste. I didn't want to insult the seer, but they were not her best batch.

Why would Ruiner give me pot brownies!?

I'm going to have a serious conversation with the man sleeping under my bed when I get back.

Shit.

I have to get back.

"I have to go," I mumble as I head for the door.

My gaze keeps lifting back to the man still leisurely leaning his tall frame against the table. A shimmering gold rune is tattooed along his crimson eye. He looks devilishly cursed. He looks like a drawing come to life. Hard lines make up his body while big eyes and charismatic smiles make up his features. The fairytales of charming princes and cunning heroes, they're written after this strange but beautiful man, I'm sure of it.

Or perhaps he'd be the villain.

"Why—why did you tell me all of that?" I ask with my hand hovering against the knob.

His shoulders lift lightly. "Because you asked. Not many people ask me anything. It's nice."

"You're a spy for the king. Surely you know better than to tell his secrets."

"I didn't tell his secrets. I told you yours."

And my secrets are that I'm a boring-ass bitch.

Why does that hurt my ego so damn hard?

"What's your name?" I ask as I open the door to a silent hall.

"Malace Hyde." His long lashes lower as he says his name. Something he doesn't seem too proud of, for some reason.

"I'm going to assume you know mine." I step out into the corridor without looking back at him, but his soft tone drifts out to me like a sad song.

"I wouldn't be a very good stalker if I didn't, Bellatrix Cuore."

I don't look over my shoulder as I rush down the

stairs of the top floor of the castle, but I feel him. I sense him now. I don't know how I ever missed his looming presence before, but he's very much like a breeze against my skin.

And I have to be very, very careful of the ghost who's haunting me.

CHAPTER TWELVE

He sits on my bed with his legs bent and spread wide. His hands fold behind his head, and he watches me intently. Malace is getting rather comfortable living in my life now. He even beat me back to my own bedroom. I close the door and fold my arms as I peer at the beautifully tragic-looking man.

"Are you dead?" I ask finally.

He's a ghost, right? He has to be.

"Don't know," he says with that same carelessness he always has.

"How did you come to the Kingdom of Carnal?"

"I've always been here."

"Since when? Since you were a boy?"

He pauses then, his crimson eyes looking into the distance like he's considering this question more in depth.

"Yes. I remember Carnal even when I was a boy."

"Could people see you then?"

Another considering pause. Then a nod. "Definitely."

"When did that stop?"

"Don't know," he says again with that same vague carelessness, and it physically pulls a sigh from my lungs. I can't exhaust myself on this man's mysteries when I have so many other things on my plate right now.

The door opens then. The hinges squeal just as Malace says one more thing.

"Do you know about the other men stalking you?"

My eyes widen and lock on him, but someone else calls out to me.

I'm sorry, what? What *the fuck*, actually?

"Bellatrix! Oh my god, I have so much to tell you!" Ivy says with so much excitement. The familiar way she says it slams into me with warmth that sears all through my heart.

In this moment, we're sisters again.

"Tell me everything!" I smile.

She bounces down on her bed, and I suddenly realize there's a man on my bed. A man only I can see. And I'm standing in the middle of the tiny room like a fucking weirdo.

I think about curling up on her bed with her like I would have done at home, but that's not the thing to do with a girl who thinks she's only known me for two days.

Stiffly, I walk to my bed. I sit at the very edge of my mattress, my ramrod-straight spine nearly brushing Malace's invisible thigh.

I don't look at him. Rule number one of not being a crazy bitch: don't acknowledge drop-dead sexy men who may or may not be ghosts.

"Oh, you have got to settle in for this! Get comfy!" Her smile is blooming, and I can physically feel my tension making this awkward.

"For sure," I say rigidly, but I move ever so slowly.

I look back at him, and his smirking eyes are watching me intently.

"Please. By all means, *get comfy*." He spreads his arms wide like an arrogant asshole.

Just when I think I'm at max capacity for asshole men in my life, one more shows up.

With jarring movements, I crawl tactfully over his legs and try to find enough room to lean against the wall. But halfway through, he grips my arm and throws me down against him. A strange little squee slips from my lips, and every single muscle in my body is tense as I lean against Malace/my pillow. The feel of our bodies touching is an electric charge. All this energy is pent up inside of him and I'm the first person to feel it seems.

"You okay?" Ivy asks slowly, her pale brows tensing together.

Malace's hands lie platonically on his thighs while I'm nuzzled right in within breathing distance of his cock.

Just let me die already. Let me die of embarrassment on this man's dick and be done finally.

"I'm great. Thanks," I clip out, trying not to let my lips graze his crotch.

"You're surprisingly warm," Malace says, distracting me even more. "I haven't felt anything like this in . . . forever."

My heart skips at the thought of that. This man's a walking, talking poem come to life. I can't handle it.

"So, Benton walked me to the class."

"Aww that so nice," I say to her through self-consciously tight lips that are most definitely not brushing against his fly.

"You're pretty with your hair fanned out like this," Malace adds, just fucking up my train of thought entirely.

I blink away his unheard input and focus on my sister's gossip.

"He's cute right?" she asks, and I desperately want to be the person she gossips to and confides in, but wow, today is just not the day. Tomorrow isn't looking great either.

"So cute!"

"Would it be strange if I touched you?" Malace cuts in.

"Yeah! Yeah, it would be."

"What?" Ivy asks.

"Right, sorry." His fingers slide soundlessly into his

palms, and it's like he's putting effort into keeping his hands to himself.

"He was waiting for me after class too," Ivy tells me with a bit less enthusiasm and a lot more confusion regarding my state of crazy.

A real smile parts my lips though. She has never had a boyfriend. I hate that she's finding a crush here, but I can't say I'm surprised. Everyone here is captivating. They draw you in without even trying. They're monstrous. But they're beautiful too. The Kingdom of Carnal may be a cruel city, but it teaches you to love unconditionally.

"Fuck, you're beautiful when you smile," the rasping, whispering poem says.

"Stop," I blurt.

"Oh. Sorry," Ivy mumbles.

"No! I meant—"

"I'm not used to people hearing what I say. I'm incredibly sorry," Malace adds.

"No. It's fine. I—I meant stop holding back and tell me more!" I smile even harder at her, and it lights up Ivy's features with her own happiness.

"I was so happy he was there, but then the king excused him."

"Leavon?" I ask, anxiety ripping through me suddenly.

"Yeah, King Leavon said I did very well in my class this morning."

"It's literally just an orientation." Everyone does

great at a fucking orientation. You can't fuck up an orientation. Why the hell is he focusing on her?

"Right. That's what I said." She blushes slightly, and I hate that I can't just explain every twisted detail to her. "He's very kind. He offered to tutor me privately when our physical training starts."

Bile burns the back of my throat.

I nod and try my best to think through the right thing to say. I want her to like me. I want her to trust me, but the trust we had is something that was built up over a lifetime. And I'm just a stranger in a kingdom of strangers to her.

"Have you heard anything about the king?" I ask instead.

"Careful," Malace whispers.

Shit. I have to be cautious what I say to Ivy, but I also have to be cautious what I say in front of Malace.

"Only that he's very accepting. Especially to, you know, people who never really felt like they belonged."

My stomach drops then.

"You . . . you didn't feel like you belong?"

Ivy was always the pretty one. The kind one. The one everyone liked.

"I just never really felt like I fit, I guess. My life wasn't terrible I just—I didn't fit in as who I really was. I felt fake. My parents worked a lot. We didn't connect. I felt . . . I felt alone. Isolated. Even when I was surrounded by people. I just wanted that family that would listen when I told them something was wrong."

My heart joins my stomach in a pit that has been dug.

She felt alone.

How did I not know that she felt like that?

"Did—did you have any siblings?"

A smile lights up her face, but it's interrupted. Confusion seeps into her big blue eyes like a fog is pushing out the light. There's a lost look in the depths of her gaze that sinks into my soul itself.

"No. I didn't."

Rage rips through me.

He fucking erased me! He made her feel alone. He isolated her and made her feel like she had no one.

Or did he?

What if I never realized just how much pain my sister hid behind her pleasant smiles?

I swallow that thought down and try not to let it show.

What if Leavon didn't isolate her? What if I did?

"I see," I say instead.

How do I connect us? How do I form a lifelong bond? How do I tell her not to trust him without telling her not to trust him?

"When I was sixteen, I had my first real boyfriend."

I feel her interest watching me. As well as Malace's.

I try my best to ignore them both and say what I know needs to be said.

"I'm so bad at picking men." My laughter sways, but it's empty. It's meant to be funny, and most people usually laugh it off. But . . . it's not funny. It's my life. And it's shit. "Even at sixteen years old, I thought he was the one. The most amazing guy I'd ever be lucky enough to say was mine."

But he wasn't mine. Not really.

"He cheated on me. For months. With everyone. My friends. My enemies. Ev-ery-one."

"What an asshole," Ivy whispers.

And this time, my smirk is real. Like I said, I'll always be at max capacity for assholes.

"He was." I nod to her. "Sometimes, the guy who comes along after the guy who breaks your heart, that guy's not the one either."

"Why do you say that?"

"Why *do* you say that?" Malace whispers from just above me.

I swallow and try to put into words the way Leavon used my hurt for his own gain.

"Sometimes, people see your weaknesses, especially when you're at your weakest, and they turn them against you. They take your trust and your love, and they prey on you." Her silence pulls at my attention, and when I meet her eyes, they're big and focused. "Always love yourself enough to protect the love you give."

I can't look away from the intense stare she's driving into my soul. Heartstrings strum like they once did when we'd stay up late talking about celebrities and boys and the cheer team she made last year.

And then she nods.

"I wish I had a big sister like you," she says as she smiles at me. My heart melts into a sappy puddle between Malace's thighs, and she's so happy, it'll just make me look even crazier if I start crying now.

A soft knock raps across the door and saves me from spilling my emotions all over ghost boy's dick. Ivy's up and bouncing to open it before I can even flail myself out of Malace's crotch.

A sad sigh sounds from behind me when I finally do lift up. I look back to see Malace staring down at his hands. He's lost in faraway thoughts, it seems.

So much so, it distracts me from the person standing in the hall.

"King Leavon asked me to accompany you to dinner tonight," Benton says.

My head turns quickly at that statement, only to find the two teens both giving shy smiles to one another.

Meanwhile, I'm the crazy bitch in the background stumbling forward to break it all up before their crush even has time to bloom.

"Dinner? In this economy?" I try to laugh it off, but my timing and terrible need to watch what I say in front of Malace is really screwing up my own fucking personality.

Shit, I'm a psycho, too, I guess.

"What?" Ivy asks with a confused laugh to accompany my own. God, now she's pity laughing. I'm ruining this friendship before it even begins.

"I—I just mean, who all will be there?" I ask, hoping like hell it's a dinner for all of the Chosen women.

"Just the three of us." Benton beams, clearly incredibly happy to spend an evening with my sister.

And the man who wants her.

Gross.

"Um . . ."

"Yeah, I'd love to!" Ivy cuts in, probably trying to shut me up before I say anything else that will embarrass us both.

"Perfect," Benton whispers. "I'll see you tonight."

They're both sending out heart eyes to one another even after the door closes.

While I'm mentally preparing myself for crashing a dinner tonight.

I hate it here.

CHAPTER THIRTEEN

THE PALE IVORY dress she wears was hand-delivered today by the king himself. He pulled her into the hall, and though I didn't hear him, I despised him anyway. The many sheer layers of it hug tight across her chest and cascade down into sparkling, golden glitter toward the hem. As she walks, it brushes along the curving sidewalk.

"You look amazing," Benton whispers.

I'm several yards back in the darkness, but I can still hear her soft laughter. I love the way it sounds. I wish—I wish like hell he was her date tonight. And not just a ruse for the Sand Man.

I stalk them in the shadows. Malace stalks me, I stalk them, and . . .

"Did you say there are other men following me?" I ask on a breath of a whisper.

"I did," Malace says as he strides casually at my

side. He looks around at the cloudy night sky as he strolls through the glowing will-o'-wisps, basked in crimson like a sinful nightmare come to life. His hands hang loosely in his pockets, his steps kicking at the winding pavement as he carries on without a care.

"Who are they?"

"Don't know," he answers lazily.

I eye him, but he's naturally oblivious.

"Would you care to find out?"

"I would, but I'm very busy with my own stalking, as you can see."

I eye him even harder. He's oblivious even harder.

Asshole.

A big, white-bricked building comes into view, and it's like I was here just yesterday. The Great Hall. Arching stained-glass windows gleam in the light of the whisking willows. I force myself not to think back to the last night I was here.

I won't think of her.

Not right now.

Benton holds the door for Ivy, and their eyes lock as she passes through. The simple look alone sends a flush through her pale cheeks.

Leavon's going to wreck her innocence.

"The side door is unlocked," Malace offers, and I'm starting to find the king's spy to be very useful.

My boots are silent on wet grass as I sneak to the darker side of the courtyard. Only to find Malace still standing silent beneath one of the dancing trees.

The pounding of my heartbeat demands I hurry up and slip inside. But his sudden behavior is so bizarre, I have to double back for him. Can't have my stalker falling behind, ya know.

Dammit!

"What are you doing!" I hiss as the sparkling red flowers illuminate our bodies. His lips part when his big shining eyes appraise every part of me in the magical ember light.

"Wow," he whispers.

Jesus-fucking-Christ, this is not the time to go all Owen Wilson on me right now!

"You're like a dream," he adds, and I seriously could slap the crazy out of this psycho right now if I thought it'd actually work.

His shining gaze drifts from my eyes to my hair, down my body, and then back again. I don't know why I fold my arms nervously across my torn shirt when he's done considering me.

"Why aren't you coming?" I say on thrusting words to try to move his oohs and aahs along a little.

"He'll know if I'm there. There's a bond of some kind between the king and me. It's not safe for you if I go in."

It's not safe for me? Since when did my stalker become my protector too?

"Oh," I say rather lamely among my hostility. "Okay." It feels weird to abandon him here like a lost dog in the great wide wilderness. "I'll meet you right back here . . ."

He nods, and his attention catches on a stray leaf that flits by in the breeze.

Shit, what if I lose him? No one can see him. He could literally be lost FOREVER.

"You'll stay right here, right?"

"What?" His head lifts, fiery eyes catching mine. It's like I can literally hear the *Jeopardy* theme song playing behind those very vacant eyes of his. The ghost of Alex Trebek is about to buzzer him any minute now.

"Stay here," I finally mutter before rushing off toward the side entrance once more. The cold gold handle against my palm opens the door with ease. It's silent, and I suddenly realize I'm concealed within a short corridor before showing the expanse of the Great Hall to the left and a smotheringly dark staircase to my right. Ivy's soft laughter trickles in from the intimately lit dining hall.

I evade the candlelit room. Instead, I take the steps two at a time to avoid being seen by not only Ivy, but possibly the king as well.

The stairs come to a landing in a balcony area that I've never been in. Several tables and chairs sit in the dark, alone and forgotten. But the gold railing ahead showcases the Great Hall below.

My sister and Benton whisper in the dark just near the door. Ahead, a single table sits at the center of the sprawling room. Two chairs are adorned with golden plates before them. A single candle with a dancing flame alights the white tablecloth.

Leavon sits there.

But he's not alone.

Ruiner shadows over the table, making it look like a dollhouse setting beneath his looming build.

"What do you mean, you don't know where the girl hails from? I'm tired of playing games with you! She was spotted with you! Are you lying, Ruiner Beaufort?" Leavon stands slowly, his fingertips tense against the tablecloth as he lifts to his slender height.

"Never, My King," Ruiner says on that deep, humming voice of his.

I sink down low then, spying between golden bars at the two men staring one another down. Ruiner could break the king with his brooding strength.

But Leavon's magic alone could kill Ruiner. I know it. Ruiner knows it. Everyone in this twisted kingdom knows it.

I still hear gossip of what he did to the Dragon King before him decades ago. That gossip alone instills fear in men as strong as Ruin.

So why would Leavon care at all about the whispers of a woman of great darkness? He doesn't need more power.

A fist slams to the table, and the shining china there clatters in fear.

"Take me to her!"

"I don't know where she is, My King."

"That's a lie. And lucky for you, I do."

"You do?" The color drains from Ruin's handsome face.

"I have more spies in this kingdom than the American world has in their fancy Eff Bee Eye," he enunciates strangely.

"God, I hope everyone starts saying it that way," I whisper to myself.

The two of them storm out of view, and I hear his words as he speaks intimately with my sister.

"Business calls, Lovely. But I do hope you enjoy the dinner tonight with your friend."

"Oh," Ivy says.

And then the door slams. Ivy and Benton wander into the center of the room, making eyes at one another even as he pulls her white velvet chair out for her.

There's literally no reason for me to stay. Aside from hiding from the king himself, who's probably raiding my room as we speak. Was that his plan all along? To get Ivy out for an hour or so to search our things. Not that I have things to search. I consider the table that's set for two. Not three.

And why would he invite Benton at all?

He wanted her out of that bedroom.

To get to me.

I stand slowly, my pounding heart calming into a deep warming as Ivy laughs melodiously once more. She deserves tonight. She deserves a fancy dress and a beautiful dinner and a good guy like Benton.

At least for tonight. Even if it is at my own expense. I turn to leave.

And come face-to-face with a stranger.

Half his skull is exposed on his left side. The bare, graying bone there startles me more than I'll ever admit. His brows wag high despite the missing flesh. A smile carves his face. And then he tackles me to the floor. Chairs rattle near my side, but I stay soundless.

"Do. Not." I gag as his fingers dig into my throat. "Fuck up. This. Date. For her."

"What?" Skull Head asks.

My knee comes up fast, and before he can curse my ass out, I'm covering his mouth with my hand and straddling across his chest.

"Shut up! Shut it up!" I hiss at him, urgently trying to save Ivy's big evening even while I'm being attacked by a fucking corpse. "Who are you?"

He flails, his arm flinging out fast, and all too fast, he hits me in the side of the face with something solid.

Stars flash behind my lids. I go down hard, and he's atop me once more.

My lashes lift, and I see stars all over again. In Synder Steel's narrowed eyes. Leisurely, he crosses into the dim lighting like a monster crawling out of a closet. Each step is meticulous.

I'm so caught up in his movements, I'm no longer focused on Skull Head. Which makes him too curious about what I'm watching over his shoulder. The corpse man flings me away and rushes my enemy. Instead of defending himself, Synder embraces the attack. His arms wrap around tight, and he literally hugs the man. Skull Head heaves his full weight into the blow to take Synder down.

Except he doesn't get the chance.

In his right hand, a glinting knife gleams in the dim light.

"You made a mistake touching her," Synder seethes, embracing the man like a friend. Even as the blade slashes out. Over and over and over again, Synder sinks the blade into the man's back. It's the relishing look in Synder's eyes that's truly terrifying. He's enjoying the feel of taking this man's life.

On the seventh stab, blood splatters out violently. The spray of it pulls a gasp from my lungs. It soaks across my chest and splatters along my face. My lips part with shock, but still I don't make a sound, even as Synder releases his hold and Skull Face drops right into me with the full weight of his very dead body.

My hands shake, but I hide it from the murderer in the room. I shove the corpse off of me and kick away with the heels of my boots, desperately putting space between me and the man who hates me. The one with the bloody knife still dripping in his hand.

He isn't a good man. The brief moment we shared in Leavon's chambers isn't even thought of when I stare up into his wild eyes.

"Get up," he rasps.

"You—you have a knife," I murmur, my voice

barely above a breath. Violent memories threaten to seep into my thoughts, but I shove them back down.

I haven't seen anyone killed since I left this place.

Fear tremors through my very bones. For the first time, I consider, maybe I should have stayed away . . .

"My favorite knife, actually." He slides it into a black leather belt around his narrow waist.

"F—favorite knife?" People have favorite knives? Like it's some kind of hobby? That's a thing?

"I said get up." His hand extends to me, and I hide my nerves as I slide my blood-soaked palm into his. "Don't ever stay on the floor. You don't belong there."

I can't keep track of his words. Two days ago, this man threatened to kill me in a crowd of people.

Tonight, he saved my life.

. . . why? Why does he keep saving me only to threaten me all over again?

The moment he has hold of my hand, I'm jerked forward. My back slams to the wall, and he covers me with the weight of his chest, his palm sliding up to cover my mouth as well. His spiraling black horns give him an impossible height on me, forcing me to angle my neck to look into his manic eyes. Adeptly, he curls one finger after the other over my mouth. He doesn't put pressure there as he breathes down on me.

"That man wanted to kill you. The longer you stay, the more other assassins will come. To. Kill. You."

I don't thrash against him. I listen.

"Other kingdoms want you dead. I—I want you gone."

Why?

He sees the flash of curiosity in my eyes.

"Leavon's a cruel king. But he also doesn't make waves. Change is what makes waves. And I've looked into you enough to know you'll cause change. No one wants that."

What does that mean?

My teeth snap out and sink into his flesh before he can pull his hand away.

His lips curl with hatred, but he slowly lowers his palm, choosing to grip my jaw instead of my mouth.

"I don't know what you think you know about me, but I can't leave."

"You will," he whispers. His fingers tighten one by one around my neck, and he lifts me with steady strength ever so slowly until my boots only minimally scuff the floor. "Nod your pretty little fucking head and tell me you'll leave tonight."

A smile carves my lips as his nails bite into my throat. I lean into him, and his stargazing eyes watch me intently for my reply. His lips morph strangely, revealing a veil of thin magic that's hiding something sinister beneath his pretty face.

"Fuck you," I whisper on a trembling breath and a smile that says I'll die with this smugness on my lips. My lashes flutter, making it impossible to hold eye contact with him long enough to call out to the magic that's lost within me.

Harder he squeezes, lifting me even higher than before.

My legs shift, but I'm still too stubborn to make a sound or disrupt the beautiful date happening downstairs. The best I can do is lift myself, my legs wrapping around him to give me a prop to lean into. My body wraps around his, my nails sinking into his forearms as I try to hold myself up by purely using his body.

I'm not stronger than him, but I know the magic I once had could help. I just have to try.

My eyes narrow on him. I lock gazes, and I try to reach that darkness that's still within me. I can feel it. I know I can do it if I just hold eye contact. I—

His hand jerks my head forward before bringing it back down against the brick wall. Blinding colors flash behind my lids. He struggles with me, his hips slamming painfully into mine to release my clamped limbs from around his lithe frame. My spine hits the wall hard, but still I don't relent. His shifting turns impatient. His palm slips against my throat, and it's then that he seems to notice the dampness there: the blood sliding beneath his fingertips.

The silver flecks in his gaze darken, and the black chases out the light until he looks up at me with big inky orbs. It's a fraction of splitting time as his gaze dances across my body, the blood, our closeness. The memory of his lips against mine flicker through my thoughts as spots of white and black sting the edges of my vision.

Rugged, desperate breaths skim against my mouth.

And then he slams his mouth violently to mine.

A single beat of uncertainty stutters through me before my lips part, and his tongue slides over mine. His hold on my throat remains, but it shifts, allowing a jagged breath to hit my lungs between his cruel, consuming kiss.

I don't know why I do it. It's the logic of considering something dangerous tangled up with the thrill of actually doing it. My heart hammers for more. The moan trembling along my tongue agrees.

My hips rock into his, and he meets me immediately. The hardness beneath his pants grinds into my core just right, and without hesitation, I slide my hands between us, shoving down the thin layer of my leggings as he continues to hold me. His hand lowers, holding the curve of my ass with one hand while keeping his threat locked around my throat.

But like a gentleman, he assists when I kick out of my leggings and panties.

And before I even realize it, his rigidness is sliding against my sex. Every defined vein and every smooth inch of him skims my wetness. He teases my clit, slipping back and forth and back and forth as he holds my gaze with narrowed eyes.

"Say you'll leave," he whispers along my cutting breaths.

My tongue glides out to wet my lips, tasting blood there as I shake my head once more.

His jaw grinds hard, his dark attention narrowing on me. His hips lift, his cock sliding lower, slipping against my opening as he continues to tighten his hold on my throat.

"You're going to leave, Bella."

"Fuck. You." I challenge him, but the moment his thickness stretches my walls, my mouth releases the weakest breath. My lashes flutter, and his rumbling laughter is all I hear as he sinks *all the way in*.

Every move he makes is meticulously slow. He thrusts into me like he wants to drag out every moment of torment between us. Instead, he just drags out every breath in my lungs and every logical thought in my head.

The angle shifts when he sinks every inch of himself into me, rocking harder at the end to drive himself as deep as he possibly can into my dripping wetness. A gasp shudders out of me, and his hand slides from my throat to my mouth, covering my sounds of pleasure with another man's blood as he does it again, and again, and again.

"That's it, baby. Tell me again how much you hate me."

My lashes lift to find hooded eyes watching me intently as he fucks me with more care and precision than any man ever has. I never knew sex could feel so good. I've never even been close to cumming with anyone in the past. How does this psychopath drive me to the edge of ecstasy without even trying? Flares of sparks alight his hungry eyes as I start to tremble. He notices each reaction his body gives me.

Even his fucking is cruel in a way. He's malevolent in the fact that he hates me. And it feels twisting and wrong to find pleasure in how he touches me.

It shouldn't feel this good to be with someone so bad.

But still, with every dragging thrust of his thickness against the deepest parts of me, that sick sensation of wrong just tangles tighter in my core. It builds and builds. I'm strung tight, and I can't help the desperate way I rock against him for more. I love it.

And I hate it.

Every thought of wrongness is washed away as the intensity in my core rises. It lifts up on a sharp edge. It's so close.

My lips part beneath his palm with jagged ecstasy just out of my reach.

And then he drops me.

His hands fall away as he steps back intentionally, slipping from me with so much quickness, an ache of anguish forms within. I feel empty and cold.

And used.

A cruel smile lifts the corner of his lips while I stare at him in confusion.

"Does it feel good?" he asks as he gives the length of his cock another slow stroke before he tucks his hardness back into his pants. "Does it feel good to know you want to fuck me and kill me all at the same time?"

The loss of my climax clears the haze from my mind as I stand nearly naked before my tormentor. He was just inside me. I let him fuck me. And he did it to mock me.

My arms fold across my chest. Humiliation stings my cheeks, but I refuse to let him know just how much he has gotten to me.

With a casual, arrogant step, he invades my space. His hand lifts, pushing back a loose strand of my dark hair along my scar. His breath skims my neck with too much intimacy. I jerk my head away from him, but he doesn't step back.

"Every man you fuck after me will never make you feel as good as I just did. I want you to think of me every time you cum and know it'll never be as good as what I could have given you." His lips press to the side of my temple before I shake away from him once more. "And if you don't *get the fuck* out of this kingdom by dawn, you know you'll end up dead. Even if I have to do it myself."

One step after the other, he backs away, his hand falling from my hair. I hold his dark glare.

I swallow to steady my tone. "You keep saying that." My voice shakes slightly, but I get the words out. "But this is the second time you've shown that you don't even have the balls to give me a climax, let alone kill me."

His lips twitch, morphing from the magic he possesses, but he covers it with a sinfully sexy smile.

"Get out of Carnal, Bellatrix. This is the last time I'll warn you."

Then he turns and leaves me.

I'm left alone and still throbbing from how he fucked me. There's an emptiness in how he left me.

Raw emotions, rage, and embarrassment sting through my chest. I shove my pants and boots back on. I storm through the dining hall, and I don't glance down at the couple sitting happily at the table below.

I won't let him get in my head. I'll prove it even. Right now.

Fuck Synder Steel.

And fuck his magnificent cock too.

CHAPTER FOURTEEN

I'm storming as well as sneaking through the corridor toward my room. When I get to the closed door, I listen intently. Silence is all that's heard. Too much time has passed since the king left the dining hall. He's long gone.

I open the door slowly to the small, dark bedroom. Unsurprisingly, I find that my bedsheet is now on the floor. The wooden bed frame is angled just slightly out from the wall.

He was here. He searched our room.

And he didn't find shit.

I shake my head at the mind games this fucking hellhole plays but I have more important things to worry about right now.

Like my orgasm.

I push the door shut, but a glinting tattooed hand

catches it at the last minute. I halt and look back at the shadowy man standing there.

Malace's crimson eyes peer at me in the dark.

"Yeah, I need a minute. Like five fucking minutes."

"I can't do that." Malace looks blankly at me, and I just know he has very specific orders he's following.

"How many times have you seen me naked?" I throw the question at him, and his brows lift high in surprise.

"I don't know. Maybe twice."

My lips curl back at that answer. "You've seen me naked?"

"Well, yeah. I'm your stalker. That's part of the job."

"I wasn't aware you were a stalking pervert!"

"I'm not a pervert!" he exclaims.

"Then give me five fucking minutes to change."

His gaze shifts back and forth in thought before he nods and steps out of the room, closing the door quietly behind himself.

Okay! I throw off my torn shirt, shake out of my pants, and kick my boots to the other side of the room. I have five minutes to prove Synder hasn't fucked with my head. Him and his meaningless cock are not something that's going to screw with my mind.

I won't let it.

I pull my cool sheet over my naked curves and settle into the soft mattress. I'm rushing, but for the love of epic orgasms, I'm going to pretend like I'm not. Everything's fine. I'm relaxed. I feel amazing.

My fingertips skim slowly down my stomach. My other hand brushes lightly across my nipple, peaking it with the barest of touch.

His kiss flickers through my thoughts, catching my breath as my fingers travel lower. Anticipation strums through me with the parting of my thighs, spreading myself as my fingers dip into my wetness.

The way his cock stretched me shudders through my core. His cruel smile sears into my mind, and my eyes flash open instantly.

"Fuck," I hiss.

"Everything okay in there?" A deeply concerned voice calls from the other side of the door.

"Shut up!" *Shut up! Shut up! Shut up!* At this point, I know I'm saying it more to myself than him. I slam my eyes closed once more for some unrushed, uncomplicated alone time.

The thing is, this kind of thing is always like this for me. It usually concludes with frustration instead of ecstasy. And when I'm with someone else, it's not much different. I'm just too in my head. It's just a problem I've always had. I'm orgasmless. I always have been. I'll never know what all the hype is about in romance novels.

Maybe I should just give up now . . .

I shake my head and try one more time to at least get *he who must not be thought of* out of my head. I pause for a second and realize the only way to do that is to think of something else.

Someone else.

The memory of how hard Ruin's slick body felt pressed against mine in the cold ocean flickers in my mind. He carried my dripping wet body from the ocean and laid me down . . .

My hand roams down my chest and stomach, and goosebumps rise as my mind runs wild.

Flashes of his hard body covering mine catch my breath. My fingers dip down to the most sensitive part of my body, my lips parting wide with the idea of him using my mouth for his big—

"Pretty Monster?"

"Fuck!" I scream, and the silence that falls into the room is crushing.

I can physically hear Malace listening at the door. Thankfully, he says nothing.

"Um—I could feel you needed me. What—what exactly do you need?" Ruiner murmurs on a hushed, gravelly voice.

"Nothing! I—nothing. Nothing. I needed nothing." The words stutter from my mouth as heat flashes across my face.

I've been naked in front of thousands of men. I've rocked my ass against their erections to the sound of an overplayed pop song and smiled coyly. I have never once, *in my entire life*, felt this level of self-conscious embarrassment.

"I can't leave, Pretty Monster."

"What?!" Go! Get out! Let me die alone of sexual embarrassment already!

"I—I know what's going on here, but until your . . . *urges* no longer require my help, I can't leave you."

My urges! Oh god! Make it stop! I feel like a four-teen-year-old boy right now having the worst conversation at the worst time with his mother.

"What do you mean, you can't go!"

"There's literally no exit down here. My magic is stalling to *help* you. I can't get out."

"Use the fucking door like a goddamn normal person and get the fuck out!"

Mattress springs squeak loudly as he seems to shift around beneath me in the dark. Seconds tick by. And then there's quiet.

"What if—what if I just helped you?"

"What!? No! The very last thing I need is—"

No man will ever make you feel as good as I could have.

A pause of dead silence passes. The man who has made my heart stupid for years is offering to—I can't even think it. How will I ever have the nerve to ask my best friend anything of the sort?

"Bella," his velvety voice rumbles across my name, and I swear, a squeak of nervousness just scurried out of me. "Do you want me to make you cum?" He says it so sensually, it floods my body with heat instantaneously. The lights are off, but my cheeks are on fucking fire.

And then I make the easiest choice of my entire life: "*Yes.*"

The entire bed shakes as dark magic I'll never understand shifts right through it. Big hands push around my hips from behind. Delicious body heat sears into me as he comes through the mattress and wraps me up in his arms. He holds me, and I lie naked against him like it's where I've always belonged.

"Should I—"

"Don't think, Pretty Monster. Just let me take care of you."

A shiver of energy rushes down my arms as his palms skim over them. He makes it so damn easy. He'd do anything for me. This isn't any different, and yet . . . it is. It's monumental, and my brain is picking apart his every move and what it means and how I should respond to each touch.

Until his lips press just behind my ear, and he breathes me in on a warm growl.

"You smell so fucking good, Bella."

My legs quake, but I try to not overthink what we're doing and what lines we're crossing in the process. The light press of his hands across my body feathers down my arms. With one palm, he skims across my breasts, one and then the other. His fingers tease there, circling my nipple, while his other hand travels lower down my abdomen. He's barely touching me, and already, I can't catch my breath. He draws faint lines across my stomach, dancing along my hips before finally inching even lower. It's then that my legs really tremble.

Without hesitation, as if he's thought of it over and over again, he parts my folds and slides right in. One finger circles my clit leisurely, pulling every jagged breath from my lungs with the slowest pace. My back arches against him, and it's just enough to hear the low groan that shakes through his chest. It's then that I realize . . . every shift I make is rocking against him. In a matter of seconds, something hard presses against the curve of my ass. My thighs press together as his cock grows even harder and larger against me.

Fuck.

I try not to think about how big he is. How thick he feels. How good he'd feel sliding into me so fucking slow—

My moan is a desperate and depraved sound as he sinks two fingers into my wetness. He's patient and gentle. With the slightest curl of his fingers, my moans crawl the walls. He does it again.

And again.

And again.

"Fuck," I cry out to the darkness.

It's then that the darkness answers.

"Bella?"

Ruiner's pace quickens. My mouth falls open. My

lashes lift. And with hooded gaze, I stare up at glowing red eyes across the room.

"Malace," I whisper on a gasp.

"What?" Ruiner murmurs with a kiss that sends shivers across my neck and arms.

I shake my head at his question, but I keep my attention held on the man leaning against my bedroom door. Maybe he *is* a ghost.

Or maybe he's an Incubus.

Because I have never in my life felt so turned on from having someone watch me the way Malace is watching me right now.

I'm spread open for him. The moon washing in through the window bathes my skin in pale light and hinting shadows. I'm a silhouette drawn for him.

And he admires every part of me.

My moan cuts off as my head tilts back against Ruin's chest, but still I hold that smoldering crimson gaze. He's a haunting of mine. He'll always be watching me.

Especially right now.

I hear it and wish like hell I could see it better. Because the shifting of jeans sliding down thighs is very apparent to me. And so is Malace's groan that follows soon after. The faint glow of golden tattoos show his sharp jaw as he tilts his head back and leans fully into the door. The shimmer of magical ruins etched along his flesh casts sinfully alluring light across hard, veering lines down narrow hips. I watch his hand stroke up.

And then down. I can't look away as he touches himself, his pace unrushed and deliberate.

"Fuck," I hiss again, my hips bucking against Ruin's palm in the best possible way.

"Good girl," Ruin murmurs against my neck. "Fuck my hand just like that."

All I hear is the melody of our breath quickening together. The three of us share this ecstasy, thriving off each other with every jagged moan we give. It's mine that are loudest though. It's an uncontrollable sound that's only quieted by Ruin's hand as he slides it up my chest, around my throat, and then over my lips.

"Ssshh, Pretty Monster." And the rumbling, needy sound of his voice as he rocks his cock against me is all it takes to send me over the edge.

His fingers never stop as I soak down his digits. He grinds the hilt of his palm against my clit, pressing hard as I thrust into his hand, and it only intensifies the shuddering sensation that's overtaking my entire body. He drags it out of me like he knows what I need even more than I do.

"I need you," I confess, my words muffled around my moans and against his hold he has on me, but I can't help but say it all the same.

I always need him. I always will.

"I know, Pretty Monster. I know," he whispers sweetly along my ear.

The trembling of my body slowly subsides, and I grow lax against him, my gaze lifting to the man still watching me intently from across the room. He holds my gaze like a dare as he continues to stroke himself, his pace quickening as his lips part. Hooded eyes lower in a wanting, tragic look.

I want to touch him. When Malace is around, I have this urge to let him feel everything he's missed out on for so long.

Especially this.

His groan rumbles through the darkness.

My eyes widen as his cock throbs in his hand. And then slickness sprays across his knuckles as he pumps himself harder and harder.

"You make me fucking crazy, Bellatrix Cuore," Malace murmurs out as he finishes himself roughly.

It's then that I realize Ruin isn't holding me anymore. He shifts from behind me. He shoves me off of him entirely as he stands with a heavy thud as his boots hit the floor.

"Who the fuck are you?"

And then he's storming directly toward the man standing against my bedroom door. The one with his cock in his hand, and his cum dripping on my floor.

Rage and murderous intent drop into the room at once, and all I can think is: I didn't even know ghosts could cum . . .

CHAPTER FIFTEEN

"You can see me?" Malace asks with wide eyes while Ruiner lifts him high and slams him down hard, rattling the door and nearly breaking it down in the process.

"I'm gonna fucking kill you, You Cock Cradling Pervert!" Eight legs stretch out deliberately from beneath Ruiner's sleek, black wings. The points of them lift with intent aimed right at Malace.

"Wait! Wait! Wait!" I'm haphazardly holding the sheet to my body as I run naked across the room. Like an offering to the spider bat gods, I throw myself in front of Malace. "He's my friend, he's my friend!" I explain.

Friend—stalker—same thing.

Ruiner's icy gaze shifts from the man he's still pinning to the wall to the woman who looks like a small child beating her fists against his broad chest.

"You let your *friend* watch us?" The sharpness of his canines on either side of his mouth snap out those words, and I can tell his anger is shifting between the both of us.

"I—I didn't think of it like that. He's a ghost. He's always around." Emotion breaks in my chest when I realize I ruined something special with the one man I trust. I barely breathe the next words out. "I didn't mean to hurt you, Ruin," I whisper on a shaking breath.

The violence in his blazing eyes softens. The pretty blue I fall into every time I look into his gaze searches my face. It takes a long moment before he finally lowers the man behind me back to the floor. My fingertips brush against his pecs, lightly skimming the heat of his scar along his shoulder.

"I'm sorry," I say on the quietest of voices, as if it's just me and him and no one else.

Just like it always is.

Gentle hands slide around my hips. His head shakes back and forth, and when he looks at me again, his attention lowers. To my lips.

He never kissed me.

He made me cum. He made me forget the cruel man who said those nasty things to me.

And yet . . . we've never even kissed.

"It's fine," he says, his rumbling voice like gravel.

"That's a relief," Malace says with a soft chuckle.

The hardness returns without delay in Ruiner's

gaze when he glares back at the man still standing behind me. I don't know how Ruin can see and feel the ghost who's been my special secrete up until now but the look of death Ruiner's gaze is more alarming than anything else.

Can ghosts die twice? If these two stick around one another long enough, we may eventually find out.

"And what's your name?" Ruiner asks, hostility dripping from his lips.

"Malace Hyde," he answers, as confused as he always seems to be in life.

A hum of thought slips from Ruiner's lips, but he shakes it away.

"The girls think that's cute?" From over my head, Ruiner side-eyes Malace's crotch with a sneer.

"It's nine and a half inches, mate. Hardly something I'd call *cute*."

The scoff that falls from Ruiner's lips is something I've never heard before. "Nine and a half. That's fucking adorable."

During their pissing contest, my mouth falls open hard as I try to make sense of just how big Ruiner's cock must truly be. It's terrifying. It's not a dick. It's a weapon. And my pussy isn't ready to be murdered.

I make a mental note to slow things way—*wayyyy*—fucking down between Ruin and me. I also make a note then and there when the sudden realization falls over me that I'm standing naked between two of the most alluring men I've ever met. Ruiner's thumbs skim back and forth along my flesh, shivering sensations all through my body. It's just enough to pull my attention back to the real issues at hand.

"You two have to go. Ivy's going to be here any minute, and I can't greet her like a nude goddess when she gets here."

Malace's brows lift high when I look back at him, his gaze rising to meet my eyes instead of my ass.

"Right," he says with an empty nod.

I slip from between them and start pulling on my clothes. When my head lifts from tying my shirt, I find both men watching me with hungry gazes.

I'm used to it. Or . . . I should be, anyway. Men would stare at my naked curves without shame every Saturday night at the club. This is no different. But then why does Ruin and Malace's attention flush heat across my face so fast?

When I'm fully clothed, I take a seat on my bed, and I curl my legs up beneath me. Ruiner's hand lifts to the door knob, but he doesn't leave immediately.

"I wanted to check on you tonight. I need you to be careful. I—I can't leave the kingdom yet, but I'll get you out of here. Soon."

He doesn't explain about the king's suspicion of me, and I don't tell him I know. I just nod to him and try not to dwell on what will happen to either of us if Leavon remembers exactly who I am.

"Just stay under the radar for the next few days, okay?"

I nod again, and he finally opens the door. Just to let it click closed. In two storming steps, he's towering over me. His hands slide down my arms, and I lift my head to him like warm sunlight is basking across my skin. Bright eyes dip to my lips. He presses a chaste kiss to the top of my head.

A held breath meets my lungs as he walks away.

He pulls the door open once more but glares to the man still lingering in my bedroom.

"You said your last name was Hyde?"

"Yeah."

He doesn't say another word. He closes the door abruptly behind him.

"He's kind of an asshole, don't you think?"

I fall back against my soft pillow and let my eyes fall closed to Malace's blunt question. The tingling sensation of what the three of us did just moments ago trembles through my body like a memory I hope I never forget.

Because we all know it'll never happen again.

The door flies open, right through Malace's body, and Ivy skips into the room with the biggest smile.

"Oh my god, Bella! I have got to tell you everything!"

"I guess I'm still mostly invisible then . . ." Malace says sadly to himself as the door is thrown through him once more and closes with a click.

I pop up from my bed, and her smile alone pulls my lips into a big grin.

"Tell me!" I demand.

"Benton kissed me!" She blurts it out with a smile that could rival the stars.

She grabs her pillow and hugs it to herself as she curls up on her bed with a dreamy look passing across her face. It fades though. That dazed happiness slips right away as she looks up at me with too much serious- ness for a thirteen-year-old girl who just got her first kiss.

"Can I ask you something?"

"Of course!" I tell her, waiting to give her the best guy advice I've got. Which according to my past shitty dating history, it's not going to be great.

"The other girls in my class, they think they're going to marry King Leavon." Her blue eyes look away from me for a moment. "They say one of us is capable of great darkness. That the king wants to find that magic within us and help us grow."

Acid burns at the back of my throat. Help them grow. He won't help them grow. He'll destroy them, one by one.

Until there's none of them left.

Discreetly, I peer up at Malace, but he's watching me closely. Does he tell Leavon everything I say? Why did I let myself get close to him when I know he holds so much power over my life?

"Tell her the truth," Malace whispers, his gaze fixed on me.

A sharp breath hits my lungs.

"The king is looking for his future queen. For decades, there have been claims great power is coming to the Kingdom of Carnal. Which can only mean that it's a newcomer. Like you. Like the other girls." I try to phrase it as nicely as I can for fear of what Malace relays to his king. "Men like Leavon, they don't wait for someone to come in and take what's theirs. They'll claim that power as their own. And they'll use it."

"Careful," Malace says under his breath, warning me of what he must do.

But I don't care anymore. I'm running out of time to care, and I won't fucking tread lightly when it comes to my little sister.

"He'll use his queen like a pawn, Ivy. Always remember that."

She nods quickly, her eyes filled with understanding as a silence crawls into the room for several passing moments.

"We can leave, you know?" I glance at her, ignoring the prying stare that Malace gives me from across the room.

Will he tell?

"No. No, I don't want to leave." She doesn't look at me, and something inside my chest crumbles. I understand her feelings.

I hate that we share that dark loathing for reality.

She's growing up just like I did. I just didn't see it before now.

"Tomorrow, our physical training classes begin." Her voice is small. Breakable. "Will you go with me?"

"Yes," I tell her without hesitation.

The memory of what those classes actually are presses into me with suffocating pressure. He named it like it's PE instead of what it truly is: *a Death Match*.

CHAPTER SIXTEEN

"Welcome, my Chosen," Leavon calls out to the crowd of not just the ten Chosen women, but all of the elite royals who linger in his kingdom, devouring the drama that unfolds. "This morning starts a new dawn of classes. Your magic will blossom beneath my watch and grow within my wisdom." Ivy peers nervously to me through the veil of her long blonde hair. My arm wraps around her side, and I pull her toward me for a half hug. Just like I used to. "Today is a physical training. Tonight, the real fun begins!" Leavon beams out to us, soaking in the manic applause.

Tonight?

My stomach twists. Physical training should last months. Nothing new should be happening so fast. Why is he rushing it?

About fifty to sixty people fill the enormous sprawling Great Hall. The single table and chairs that were set out last night have been swept away. Probably to the upstairs, but honestly, who fucking knows. They could be stored in Leavon's arrogant asshole for all I know or care.

"So let us begin! And let your elders guide you and help you!" he adds with a dramatic sweep of his hand.

As he steps back, I see a dark figure at the back of the room. Standing as far away from Leavon as he possibly can is Ruin. Big black wings shade his brutish good looks. His narrowed eyes catch mine, and if he were any closer, I'd swear I could guess what he'd say in that brooding, rumbling voice of his: *when I said to stay under the radar, is this what you thought I meant?*

My gaze averts quickly.

A group of three girls rush out to the middle of the room, clearly excited to show off whatever magic they've gained in the last few days. The rest of the Chosen women spread out a bit slower, less confidently. While the others watch with hungry eyes for the show to begin.

"You shouldn't be here," a mysterious voice whispers to me from over my shoulder.

My head turns, and he's too damn close. My cheek nearly brushes his as I look into those starry eyes.

"Fuck off, Synder," I tell him through tight lips, not letting my mind wander to the things we did last night in this very room.

"Funny, I'm pretty sure I said the same thing to you

recently. And yet, here you are. Still in my fucking kingdom."

His kingdom. The arrogance of this man.

"You know the others here, they're meant to challenge the Chosen. They're meant to set an example." He brushes against my back, trembling heat all along my body. "Set an example with me, Bellatrix."

I eye him once more, and his presence just behind me is even closer. It's a challenge. He won't kill me, but he wants to put me in my place all the same.

Too bad I won't give him the chance.

"I'm busy." I trail after Ivy, giving her space and freedom, but also, ya know, helicoptering around for any crazy Chosen bitches who might try their magic on her.

To my surprise, she makes her move rather quickly. Her small stature gives her an advantage to sweep around the room without drawing attention. She zigzags through the wrestling and zapping magic soaring through the Great Hall. In a matter of seconds, she's leaping on the largest woman in the room. The woman's muscles bulge in her biceps when Ivy climbs her back and wraps an arm around the woman's windpipe. I stop walking and focus intently on the little girl I grew up with. The girl everyone babied all her life.

And then red smoke drifts from her lips. She whispers unheard words into the girl's ear like a song that only she knows the lyrics to. Little by little, the large woman's knees give out. As if she's fighting against something unseen, the woman drops to the floor. And slowly keels right over into heavy unconsciousness. There's a happy, glinting sparkle in my sister's eye when she gazes down on the full-grown woman whose gaping mouth has now given way to deep snores.

"*Shittt*," someone says in astonishment from over my shoulder.

My slitted gaze shoots to the asshole who once more is shadowing over me. Why do I feel like I have an abundance of stalkers in my life at the moment? One obnoxious man in my life is more than enough.

"Looks like your pet project doesn't need you looking after her." His words skim along my shoulder, his head dipping low as if he might taste me there. "Show me you're more than just sweet thighs and devious lies."

Deep dark eyes challenge mine, neither of us daring to look away for several heated seconds.

And then my arm snatches out quick, slamming my fist into the dead center of his throat. A coughing, gagging gargle is his new snarky reply, and the smile on my lips is a slicing weapon as I use the pained distraction to sweep his knees out from beneath him.

He goes down hard, blooming confidence all through my chest with how easy it was.

I kind of missed this. It's fun. It's exhilarating. It's—

My legs give out without warning. I'm flat on my back, choking on my next breath in the span of a single second.

"You look good lying on your back, baby," he whispers to me as his thighs straddle over my arms and chest. A long finger strokes the edge of my jaw as he appraises me struggling under his weight. "You look even better beneath me."

Cruel lips twitch with veiled magic. His mouth moves unnaturally as violence takes over his galaxy eyes, turning them into inky wells of sin. That darkness fully takes over. His smile becomes animalistic. His mouth morphs, stretching across his sharply jagged teeth. He could devour me, bite my head clean off. Maybe he will . . .

"You're a Shapeshifter," I accuse, knowing very well that his magic is hiding an even more sinister appearance than he has revealed.

"A Phuca actually." The confident way he says that has me wracking my brain for the meaning of that creature but nothing comes to mind. "Show me what the Fae think is so damn special about a mortal bitch like you," he says through that eerily stretched mouth of his. "What are all these kingdoms whispering about? You're not the one, Bellatrix. You're not."

My boots kick against the cold tile flooring, my arms flailing at my side as dark memories surface from this very room. Her screams and the look of dead terror in her eyes are louder than the sharply spoken words of the man holding me down.

Melissa was so kind to me. She was my only friend. And I killed her.

Pain shoots through my heart, snapping me out of the past and bringing me fully to life in the present.

He has pinned me. You can see it in his death-black eyes: he thinks he has all but won. Except . . . he doesn't know. He doesn't know who I was when the Sand Man made me into the Monster I am today.

I lock eyes with him. The darkness within me rears up. It sears right through me with shaking power.

The air in his lungs can't escape. Oxygen can't get in either. Which is strange. Because to the viewers around us, he's breathing fine. Not a single thing has changed between he and I. Unless you count the cryptic thoughts that keep flashing into his mind. They're scratching in like fingernails digging into his brain. I'm gripping hold of his every thought as I force in the image of me climbing on top of him. He lies flat beneath me with his hands held high on either side of his pretty, terror-ridden face.

As for me, I sit straddled over him rather lazily. I cross my legs to get comfortable. I pick at my clean nails. Not a muscle twitches through his hard body while I don't lift a single one of mine.

And yet, I paralyze him with fear.

"My magic is that of a sleep demon. I trained for a year to master their darkness. People like me, we send our victims into a state of paralysis," I tell the sexy man as I sit atop his useless body, weighting him down in a crippling pain of immobility. "I like you like this, Syn.

You're cute like this. Maybe you should stay like this. *Forever*."

The crippling fear of his new life I've gifted him has faded away the darkness that shifted his features into a Monster. His lips turn full and human again. Only his curved black horns remain.

The threat he tormented me with last night circles my mind, and a smile parts my lips as I lean in sweetly. My cheek brushes his, and I whisper into his ear.

"Just know, no other woman will ever terrify you the way I have. No one will ever make you feel as weak as I have. I fucking own you, Synder Steel."

An empty breath shudders from his lungs, coming out jagged across his dry lips.

And then I cut the trance.

He falls off of me, curling up at my side as he fights desperately to get a full breath. The crowd parts for us, giving the man space and eyeing the woman who never lifted a finger against him. Murmurs start to spiral through the room.

"How did she do that?"

"Who is she?"

"Is she a Chosen?"

Actual worry crawls in as I sit up slowly . . .

Shit.

I was supposed to stay under the radar.

My lashes lift, and when they do, Ruin is staring right at me. And so is Ivy.

And so is Leavon.

177

CHAPTER SEVENTEEN

I RUSH THROUGH THE COURTYARD, never once looking back. The red glow of the will-o'-wisps feels like an omen when their blood-red light casts across my face. The clouds above rumble with rain that hasn't yet fallen. It shakes through my chest like my own feeble heartbeat. The doors of the castle are just up ahead, but the more my mind races, the more I realize, I can't go back. As much as I want to be as close to Ivy as I possibly can to protect her, it's not safe for either of us if I go back there.

I won't leave her either though. Especially knowing that the festivities begin tonight.

My steps stagger as I run out the gold gates and find myself on the cobblestone streets of Carnal City. Every person I pass makes me wonder if they know. The more I'm seen, the more the king will have intel on me.

How do I know I'm not being followed right now?

I resist the urge to fully spin in a fucking circle like a crazed ballerina to ensure I'm safe. Instead, I peer tactfully over my right shoulder.

No one's there. Yet.

Or are they?

Jesus fuck! This city has made me insane!

Someone jars into my shoulder, and that's all that's needed to set me into a full state of panic. At the first door I come to, I fling it open and close it quickly behind me. The little cottage is identical to the one Ruiner shared with me the first night I came to Carnal.

He let me sleep on the little cot on the far wall. He made hot tea from the firestone at the center of the home. Aside from the small bed and fireplace, only a table and one wooden chair reside within the circular room.

I can't stay here for long. The Brotherhood keeps no secrets from their king. Every secret Ruiner's ever kept for me whispers through my thoughts, but that's not the point. If I'm found in the home of a Brotherhood, they'll report me at once.

I push out the thin shutter from the window a fraction of an inch. Its hinges give way with an angry, shrill sound that has my heart trembling with anxiety. The window is just a small circle, barely larger than my head, fitting the aesthetic of the little adorable cottage perfectly. I can't push the shutter open much, or I'll draw unwanted attention. The road outside is a mess of people milling about. Through the thin slit of the opening, I can see all the tradesmen and hustlers doing their daily deals. It won't be any less crowded when nightfall comes.

Especially on a festival night.

A deep breath enters my lungs, and I start a counting process to calm my nerves. Another big breath, and I'm starting to feel steady. Another one and my hands no longer shake at my sides.

Somewhere between the fourth and tenth breath, the fucking door flings open.

The sunlight blinds the figure into an intimidating silhouette. His horns reach up, threatening to slice open the heavens with his towering height alone. With his next step, his features are revealed and captivating, starry eyes now glare my way.

"Moth-er-fucker," he whispers to himself.

I yank the window closed with a loud clack. My wide eyes never look away as he walks fully in with a smile cutting across his lips and very casually pushes the door closed behind him, *blocking the exit*.

An unsteady tremble catches my hands. I fist my fingers hard into my palm to stop the anxiety from rising back up. Mentally, my mind is racing to access all the possibilities of how I can wound him. But there's nothing of use in the little home. Unless I can somehow shove a chair up his ass and run away, I'm fucked.

"I've never met someone who had such an affinity for dying, Bellatrix," he says, striding into the room one step after the other like an animal about to strike. As he comes closer, his hands drop to his black belt, the one that holds more knives than I can even see. Casually, he unhooks the clasp there. He pulls the leather through the loops and drops it on the chair just near the window. Far too close to me for my liking.

My mouth turns dry, and it isn't lost on me that I just embarrassed a shapeshifter in front of the highest noblemen in this kingdom.

I follow his movements as he reaches behind his horns and pulls. The white shirt inches up along every hard line of his torso until he pulls it off entirely. Ever so casually, he pushes off his boots. And then his hands drop once more to his waist, his eyes glinting viciously as he holds my gaze.

His black pants lower, and he steps out of them. He's nude before my very eyes, and I can't look away as a thousand terrible thoughts rip through my mind.

Real fear drops into me. Every man I've ever met has hurt me in some way or another. Synder Steel is no different.

And he's about to prove that in the most violent way.

"W-what are you doing?" I mumble without that normal false confidence that I cling to so damn hard. Without a word, he comes closer, closing the distance between us until there's nothing left. The slamming of my heart fills my ears. My breath comes in shaking inhales that don't seem to ever reach my lungs.

His gaze softens just slightly as he looks down on

me. It isn't a look of kindness. It's a look of defeat. The crack of light through the window reveals his starlit eyes, and there isn't an ounce of darkness within them.

There's exhaustion.

"I'm fucking going to bed."

He passes me then, his smooth shoulder brushing mine and catching my eye with the golden tattoo that gleams there along his flesh.

I blink through my messy thoughts.

"I—You're going to bed?!" I ask, astounded, as if I'm heartbroken he isn't going to totally mutilate, murder, and use my body as a new, fun raincoat for this stormy island.

"Yeah. It's been a shitty few days. I'm tired. I'm going to bed."

"Um—" I consider what the fuck that leaves me to do, then . . .

If Synder and I aren't constantly at each other's throats, we have no idea what to do with one another. Where do I go from here?

Should I leave? Hide in the forest until I figure out a plan? I'd have to get to the forest unseen for that to happen.

Not likely.

"Can I stay here?" I awkwardly ask my arch nemesis.

He pulls the heavy covers over his lean frame and turns in toward the wall. Only the hard lines of his muscular back are consoling me in this moment.

"I literally do not fucking care. Whether you stay or leave, that's not my fucking problem anymore."

I arch an eyebrow at his flippantness.

"You've threatened me every single day like a little inspirational quote-of-the-day calendar." I lean into the wall and give his sexy back my full attention. "What gives?"

He flings up so fast, it shakes the nerves right through me. I smooth my hands on my leggings and try not to look terrified of being in such a small space with such a total psychopath.

"Because they all know! Leavon, the Fae Kingdom, everyone, Bella! There's no hiding it. A change is coming. And we're fucked because of it!"

His jaw ticks as he glares up at me with more hate than I've ever seen gleaming in his eyes before. His smooth chest rises and falls with fury shaking through his every breath.

"I'm not here to make change. I'm not that person. I'm not the Chosen."

His lips twitch with veiled magic, but he covers it with a cruel, kissing smile.

"How many women have survived out of the hundreds that have been chosen for the king?"

I shrug my shoulders.

"How should I know?"

"Just you," he whispers, his gaze slipping to the floor between us. "In twenty-four years, only you have survived. Do you think that's a coincidence?"

"Twenty-four years?" The breath falters in my chest as that number slams into me hard. I just turned twenty-four three months ago.

"Yeah." His voice isn't calmer, but it's quieter, laced with a hint of fatigue.

"What happened twenty-four years ago?"

His brows lift as he looks at me from beneath thick lashes. He stares for so long, it seems to occur to both of us how little I truly know of this hellish kingdom.

"Leavon killed the Dragon King. He crowned himself ruler. And the Darkness of this kingdom has never been the same since. Instead of helping us, the magic has hindered us, twisting us into Monsters not even our mothers could love." He seems to take a careful moment to think through his words before speaking again. "Everyone says if he's replaced, if someone powerful enough replaces him, our magic will be cleansed, no longer cursed by his greed. And the Kingdom of Carnal actually prospering, that scares the shit out of the surrounding kingdoms. People don't like change, Bella."

"You'd rather be cursed than prosperous?" I ask with an astounded sneer.

"Yeah. We would. We'd rather be cursed than dead. Because if we're a threat of power to the Fae Kingdom, they'll come for us. And we won't win." His galaxy eyes are swarming with mania, and I don't know how to calm this man when he's not trying to kill me.

I don't even know why I want to.

"I won't make change. I don't want that." The fate of an entire kingdom? Who the hell wants that kind of responsibility?

"You're such a fucking blind optimist, you can't even see that you don't get a goddamn say in it, Bellatrix."

I swallow hard at that.

What if he's right? What if I am the Chosen? How am I supposed to be what these people need? Especially if they don't even want it?

"I'll leave," I whisper.

He shakes his head at me, his hands shoving through his messy, blonde locks until he meets the curve of his black horns.

"I'll leave tonight. Right after the festival." I nod once with conviction, trying to make a plan to get Ivy to come with me.

I can do it. I'll save us both. And then I won't have to worry about screwing up an already screwed-up kingdom.

"Just . . . get some sleep." He pulls back the thick blanket of his cot and scoots over to the wall. "You'll need it."

He's still holding the blanket back for me. My eyes shift to the left and then to the right, anywhere but at his dick that's now being revealed to me like a grand prize I never asked to see.

"Um . . . I—What?"

His lips pull at the corner with a devious smile.

"You've let me eat your pussy and fuck you crazy but taking a nap with me is where you draw the line? Prude."

I close my eyes to focus on just my thoughts and not his cock that's growing harder as we speak. Someone spritz it back down with a spray bottle before I make any more bad decisions in my life.

"I don't sleep with men who try to kill me day in and day out."

"No, you just fuck them."

My jaw tightens as I open my eyes to glare down on him.

Why is his smile so fucking sexy right now?

"The festivities will last until dawn tomorrow. You'll need to be ready if you plan to survive them without being claimed by the King by the end of the night."

My foot taps impatiently for me to make the decision to either crawl under his warm blanket or run out the fucking door screaming. I blow a long, pent-up breath from my lungs to get the lock of hair out of my face as I give him my most serious look.

"I want the pillow between us at all times."

"Will there be room for it with all that lustful tension that already lies between us?"

I bite my cheek hard.

"Pillow! Now!"

"Okay, but it's pretty thin. I can't promise that it'll hold much back between us." His taunting smile is so fucking gorgeous, I want to slap it off his arrogant face.

He slides the white pillow down his abs. It's the slowest push of his palm traveling down before it finally covers cock.

Shit. Why do I have the intense urge to be reincarnated into this man's pillow in my next life?

If I'm being honest, a little slut bus voice at the back of my mind is crying to see him covered up.

Stiffly, I sit at the edge of the mattress. I kick my boots off much less gracefully than he did. I look up at the door and wonder if there's still time to go running screaming into the streets.

A crack of thunder shakes the thin walls. Then the sound of rain pounds against the rooftop.

I guess that's the finale of our little argument.

He wins.

And though I won't say it to his face, he's right. I should get my rest before tonight. I'll need it.

My legs slip in, and I don't face him as I take his kind offering.

Synder Steel will always be an enigma to me. He's the cruelest man I've ever met. And yet he continues to find kindness to show me.

There are several moments that slip in without a word between us. His warmth seeps into me, and the mattress shifts as he exhales and with that very breath, he seems relaxed.

He's relaxed around me.

"I don't trust you," I whisper.

A beat passes before he turns toward me, his breath wafting along my neck in such a way that I physically ache to feel him. He doesn't hold me like Ruin would. He doesn't bring me calming energy.

He brings total fucking chaos.

But something does feel like it's shifting between us.

"That's good, Bellatrix" he whispers, his words fanning my flesh as he presses a slow, faint kiss to the back of my neck. He turns away from me to find sleep, but he whispers one last threatening warning to me before he does: "You shouldn't."

CHAPTER EIGHTEEN

Booming laughter breaks way through the lulling sound of heavy rain. My lashes lift to the darkness of the room, and for a moment, confusion is all I have to grasp on to.

The memory of Synder's cottage comes flooding in as more partygoers outside holler and howl with amusement. Excitement. Bloodlust.

It's festival night.

I push back the warm blanket off my body, and I realize how incredibly rested my mind feels. Have I slept all day? Jesus, do I really find that much comfort in Synder Steel's bed?

What is wrong with me?

A dwindling fire spreads heat and dim lighting through the circular room. The window I peered out earlier is now locked with a heavy chunk of wood slid across its steel barricade brackets. A bowl and spoon sit in front of the chair. Unused.

Synder isn't here. He hasn't been for a long while if the fire is any indication.

Did he lock me inside his home? Has he gone to the king? My bare feet pad across the cold wooden flooring. The moment my hand turns the knob and it doesn't give way, my fragile heart stutters.

"Shit!" I hiss.

The floorboards shake when I rush back to the other side of the tiny cottage. I pull my boots on roughly, and within seconds, I'm at the shutter windows once more.

But its petite size that I once thought was so damn adorable is infuriating now. It's too fucking small for me to fit through!

Dammit!

Why did I let my guard down around him? Why did I think things were different between us now? Why was I so fucking stupid to trust the pretty man with a smile like the devil and the horns to match!?

They're coming for me. They're coming for me, and now I won't even be able to protect myself, let alone Ivy!

Metal scrapes against metal, and the door knob turns so slowly, I think I'll die of heart failure before I ever give these bastards a chance to capture me alive. At the last second, I grip the metal spoon in my fist and round the fire, hunching myself down on the blind side of the swinging door that's opening. I feel for the magic within me. It lifts in my chest with a sense of reassurance. My muscles string tight. I'm ready.

I'm not strong enough to kill the four members of the Brotherhood and Leavon. But I'll die trying.

Sleet crackles louder before the door's pushed softly closed. It's closed much sooner than I anticipated for a brawl between so many people.

And that's because only Synder stands there, his piercing eyes narrowing on the spoon that's now bent in my tightly held fist.

"What, ah, what are you doing, Bellatrix?" His golden eyebrow arches mockingly at me.

A satchel hangs in one of his hands, a long loaf of bread sticking out the top. In his other hand, he carries a white box.

None of his knives are out and ready for the bloodbath my mind had created for funsies. In this strange moment with his hands full of shopping bags and boxes, he's as threatening as a soccer dad carrying in a trip of groceries.

"Um—Nothing. Nothing." I casually try to straighten back out the spoon, but it doesn't help me in the least, remaining U-shaped for both he and I to look at pathetically. "Sorry," I whisper awkwardly as I stare down at the poor state I've left his eating utensil in.

"You'll really be sorry when you have to eat the soup I brought you with that thing."

Soup? He brought me soup?

It's poisoned! my little crazy mind warns me. At this point, if it is, I can only hope it takes me out before I have time to embarrass myself any further.

He lays out a slightly damp loaf of bread. A small knife I haven't seen before is pulled from his black belt. With care, he cuts off the wet end and sets it aside before slicing two precisely cut pieces. Then he brings out a small jar with a red ribbon adorning the top. It opens with a clatter, and with the same knife, he spreads what appears to be butter across the pieces of bread. I'm in a trance as I watch him work so mundanely but so manically as well. He wipes his knife on his jeans with care before sliding it back in its place with the others.

And then my nose takes in the warmest smell as he pulls out a covered bowl from the bottom of the bag.

"I didn't know what you liked, but chicken noodle soup is Chef Cecelia's specialty."

Have I fallen into another psychotic realm? Is this shit actually happening right now? Who the fuck is this guy, and what has he done with the asshole I was just getting used to?

A fresh white napkin is laid to the right of the bowl of wafting, hot soup. The perfectly cut slices of buttered bread are set nearly atop the napkin.

And then he steps back as if to unveil it all for me.

"Um—" Do I eat it and face sudden poisonous death . . . or do I really have the impolite balls to turn down all this? "It smells delicious," I whisper before taking the seat he has pulled out for me.

Christ! This is how people pleasers die: It would be rude to say no to poisoned soup.

But the thing is, if Synder wanted to kill me, he could have. Sev-er-al times. He murdered a man in cold blood right in front of me. He has never actually tried to kill me. He has just tried to get me to leave.

Hot noodles slide over my lips, and I audibly moan. My eyes close as I take another big bite. Chef Cecilia is a Goddess!

My lashes open slowly, and those galaxy eyes of his are watching me intently. It isn't a glare for once. It's a look of curiosity. Interest.

Things are definitely weird between us now. It isn't fucking that changed things between us. It's the other f word: friendship.

"You've mentioned the other kingdoms a lot." I pry the best I can without flat-out asking if he's a double agent spy for both Leavon and the Fae.

He hums a noncommittal reply before turning his back on me and opening the white box on the tangled blankets of his bed. He's as good at avoiding me as he is at stalking me.

Definitely a spy.

"The golden tattoo on your arm, what does it mean?" I try instead.

"It's the symbol of the Brotherhood." He's quick to answer that one, and so I carry on with that topic.

"Every member of the Brotherhood has one?"

"It's an honorary rune the King of Carnal has marred his Brothers with for centuries. Nothing is thicker than blood. Except magic."

I consider the identical rune Malace has. I know I've seen it on him.

He was a member of the Brotherhood . . .

Where is Ruiner's tattoo?

Before I've had time to lick my bowl clean, Synder pushes aside the last layer of tissue paper and pulls out a long, sweeping gown. He turns with the shimmering, lacy dress in hand, revealing it to me the same way he did the soup.

At some point, I'm going to have to stop gaping at this bizarre imposter and just accept him as Synder 2.0. He's much better than the previous edition. This one comes with an actual personality.

"What the fuck is that?" I ask bluntly instead of people pleasing my ass over to him with a mouth full of thank-yous.

Extravagant gowns are apparently the limit for my people-pleasing trust.

"You'll need a gown for tonight to blend in. Leavon will spot you instantly if you stride in there with your tits bouncing around a shirt that he personally tore off of you.

Ahhh, there the old Synder is. To think I was starting to miss him.

I swallow down my snarky reply and force my

tense lips to say the words. "Thank. You."

Yep. Don't like that. Not one bit. Feels fucking unnatural to thank this asshole.

He walks into the light of the fire, and tiny gemstones gleam around the thin emerald lace of the sleeves and neckline. The material changes there into a simpler fabric that hugs across the chest and flares out dramatically at the hips.

"It's beautiful," I admit on a hushed tone.

"It matches your eyes," he tells me, his fingers sliding down the front of the gown in such an intimate way that I find myself shivering from the thought of his hands against my body.

What is wrong with me? Was the soup actually poisoned with stupidity? Get a grip, Bella!

He hands it to me then, and the fabric alone has me rubbing the sleek feel of it between my fingertips. I've never worn something so gorgeous. I was a mess my last two years of school. After the Sand Man incident, I didn't try anymore. I secluded myself. I didn't make friends, and I definitely didn't attend prom.

What does it feel like to be the girl in the pretty dress? To have the guy gaze at you like you're a princess come to life?

A gaze . . . that's nothing like the hungry look Synder is sending my way as he leans against the table, arms crossed, waiting.

"Turn around." I lift my head high at the demand. He cocks his head in confrontation.

"Why? Think I might see something I haven't already?" His long fingers tap against his bicep, and I want to punch his pretty face until that cruel smile finally fades away.

My lips purse, but before I can release the pent-up anger on my tongue, his smirk parts with a long, melodious laugh. And then he turns around, facing the door rather casually.

He listened to me. Should I sneak back to my bedroom at the castle for a Reality Ripper? Maybe that will fix all this weirdness between the two of us.

I rush as I undress. It's a race to shove out of my leggings. It's almost like I'm afraid he'll change his mind last minute, and I'll find myself trying to fight him in just my underwear.

Again.

But he doesn't attack me. He doesn't peek over his shoulder or make me uncomfortable at all, really.

"I'm not a spy, by the way." His voice carries along the walls, and I look up as I'm stepping into the puddle of pretty material at my feet.

"What?"

"You were suspicious of the information I have on the Fae Kingdom. I'm not a spy."

"Oh," I say. Because what can I do but wait for more? It's like he feeds me. He's giving me little pieces of this broken, psychotic man, and all I want is to have all the jagged parts all gathered up in my arms to keep safe from anyone else.

"My mother is Fae. So are my brothers. They send me messages every day. Even when I don't reply."

Why wouldn't he reply?

"What do the messages say?" I ask, my arms sliding into the fine jade lace.

His throat clears harshly. Seconds pass in the dimly lit room, accompanied only by the heavy tapping of the rain.

"They say they've heard the rumors of the great darkness that's coming. It has made them anxious. They say the Fae won't hesitate to strike The Kingdom of Carnal down if Leavon marries."

"Why?' I breathe out.

"Because Carnal was once on the brink of prosperity. A Dragon King far stronger than Leavon was rebuilding what centuries of poverty had destroyed." His head shakes hard. "Poverty kills. Enough time has passed to show that our race is dwindling, hanging by a thread. The Fae hope that thread snaps. And then they won't have to think about the tainted race of Monsters they abandoned to this island such a long time ago."

I'm blinking at his lithe silhouette. The hurt in his tone is rawer than I've ever heard. The Fae are his family. And they're not kind to him.

"Um—" I pause with uncertainty, and he peers just slightly over his shoulder at me. "Could you lace up the back?" I nod toward the back of the heavy gown that's hanging loosely at my shoulders.

Starry eyes take me in for a long, drawn-out

moment. My thighs shift from the heat of his stare. My heartbeat storming in my chest doesn't sound like the weak heart my mother always warned me about.

It sounds powerful and demanding.

I turn as he crosses the room, and anticipation thrums all through me. Seconds pass with the firelight dancing across the wall.

Still he doesn't touch me.

I've never wanted to feel someone's hands on my body as much as I do right now.

Gentle fingers skim down my spine. Tingles race after his touch, and the breath in my lungs has long been forgotten. Soft strings tickle along my flesh before he pulls tight. I'm jerked against his chest, and that breath that I'd forgotten falls across my lips in the form of a lusty gasp.

My lashes lift as I look up at him from over my shoulder.

And then he smiles.

"You really do like it when I tie you up, don't you, baby?"

My eyes roll hard, and I have to mentally tell myself to take a step forward and stop melding my body into his sexy chest like a needy cat.

His quiet laughter is so tender, it warms my heart though.

Is he letting his guard down around me? Or maybe deep down, he just likes to take care of people. Take care of me.

The material of the gown presses into my chest until my breasts are pushing against the pretty, shimmery lace at the upper half. I feel him working and with every move of his hand, my waist looks more slender and yet curvy all at the same time.

"Done," he whispers along my neck. His breath is shallow, teasing my skin in a way that makes my lashes flutter hypnotically.

I take a step away from him before turning around to watch the beautiful hem line swirl around my unseen feet.

It's beautiful.

"You're beautiful," he says like a confession even he didn't expect.

When our eyes meet, there's a magnetic charge sparking the space between us. I can't look away. My feet move of their own accord, taking me to him without thought. I've never wanted anyone as much as I want Synder Steel in this moment.

Then a bang slams through the room. A cold wind shivers across my skin, and I nearly drop to my knees and thank god for the interruption of Benton standing in the dark doorway

Logic comes crashing in my mind, reminding me that this man is not a good man.

Benton freezes when he sees me so close to his brother. My face flashes with heat that I hide by dipping my head low to let my hair slide in front of my features.

He rushes past me and is toe-to-toe with Synder in less than a second.

"Are you out of your mind? What is she doing here? Alone. With. You." Benton pauses just long enough for Synder to open his mouth but not long enough to let him speak. "You saw the way Leavon looked at her! Do you have a death wish?"

"Did you bring what I asked for?" Synder ignores the rush of warning Benton gives him, including the astounded stare he's still pinning him with.

"Yeah." Benton reluctantly extends his hand and offers a small bag to his brother.

"Put these on." A pair of black high heels and a stark black cloak are shoved my way. "And take this," Synder adds, hiding something in his palm that really spikes my curiosity.

"What is it?" I ask with hesitation for the very first time this evening.

"Realipine. Most of the people in Carnal grow immune to it rather quickly. We have to find other drugs to block out the madness at night but it should still work for you."

Ah, yes. Reality Rippers do have a formal name. One I've already forgotten what it was by the time I've swallowed down the tiny dry pill.

My trust in this guy is officially at a worrisome level. If me from two days ago could see me now, she'd kick me in the vag for even standing this close to Synder Steel, let alone taking drugs from him.

My height teeters in the heels that are most definitely the tallest pair I've ever worn. I'd normally avoid shoes like this for fear of accidently impaling the male ego with my slim, five-eleven frame.

Still, when I step into the soft cloak Synder offers, he towers over me by several inches, not including his spiraling black horns.

"Perfect," he whispers against my neck.

When I turn to him, I have the impossible urge to step into him and press my lips to his just to see if this violent man would be as gentle with our kiss as he has been to me all night.

"It's nearly midnight," he tells me like I'm a true princess I've read about all my life. The spell breaks entirely, though, when my prince speaks again. "You should go."

I feel Benton watching us. Nothing else matters in this moment though. My heart's knocking hard for me to make a move that I won't get another chance to make in this wicked kingdom.

Aching pain strikes through my chest when I turn my back on him. I can't start something I'll never finish. This isn't a fairytale. Synder isn't a good guy. And I'm most definitely not a princess.

I have to go.

Because when dawn comes, I'll be gone. Just like he wanted.

CHAPTER NINETEEN

THE STORM BREAKS. Soft rain pitter-patters along my cloak by the time I reach the courtyard of the castle. The wind smells of the sea. Crimson colors light my path toward the Great Hall as the limbs of the will-o'-wisps dance around the hundreds of people milling about.

The hood of my cloak is pulled tight against my billowing gown, but I can still peer around slightly. I search the entire way there, but I never do spot Ivy.

But someone familiar does come into view.

Ruiner stands on the far side of the building, his wings covering the frame of a man whose golden tattoos illuminate them both. To only confirm my suspicions, everyone who passes Ruiner looks at him like he's lost his damn mind . . . for yelling at someone who only he can see.

Poor guy. Can't catch a break in this hellhole of a kingdom.

Casually, I stride up to the pair of total opposites.

"I'm not him!" Malace says adamantly as I get closer. "Whatever you think you know is wrong."

"Hello?" I ask, hating that I'm interrupting a very important argument.

The moment Ruin locks eyes with me, he shifts , spreading his wings wider to hide me from the view of the guest filing into the hall.

"What are you doing here?" Ruin seethes.

"Wow," Malace whispers, his eyes lit up like his gaze itself owns the sun. His attention dips to the ribbon of the cloak that ties against my lacy cleavage. The fabric mostly covers the birthmark there, but Malace seems to find it anyway. He doesn't look at it like it's strange. He looks at it like it's a beautiful memory.

Ruiner's glare slices toward my friend, but despite his rage, he says nothing to Malace's dreamy attention.

"He knows. It's not safe for you. Let me take you home. Please, Bella," Ruin says so intimately, I want to sink right into him. I want to give him everything he wants.

But I can't give him that.

"I—my sister is here, Ruin," I finally confess. It's a weight of a secret that I've been hiding from him. "She doesn't remember me, and I don't know how to fix that, but I'm leaving tonight. I just can't leave without her."

"Ivy," Malace guesses, and once, more Ruiner glares at him like his voice alone turns Ruiner murderous.

Leathery wings shuffle around me with the chill of the wind picking up, and it takes him several moments to finally reply.

"We'll have to get Leavon to lift whatever repression rune he's placed on her to forget you. Once he has done that, she'll remember everything he has repressed. If he doesn't lift it, she'll never remember." Ruiner's plotting really swings into effect as he thinks it over at a rapid pace. "Find your sister during the festival and get her to show you somehow where the rune is. Only powerful magic can revert rune magic. We'll have to find someone if Leavon won't do it himself."

All the information trickles into me, but I'm still caught up on one thing and one thing only:

"Where's your mark of Brotherhood?" I ask Ruiner.

His brows lower at my question, but he turns for me. His wings lift high, arching above his big body like he's a dark god. Eight thin black tendons line his spine, pulled in and arching along the sides of his back. They're like a cage in appearance, but they're much more deadly than they appear. And there, at the center of his spine, is a glowing, golden mark.

Just like Synder's.

As I suspected, Malace's brows lift high at the sight of the familiar ruin.

"I know that mark," he says slowly.

"It's the mark of the Brotherhood. Anyone who has ever shared the bond of Brotherhood has this mark." I watch him as confusion seeps into his crimson eyes.

"I have that mark," Malace whispers sadly.

He lifts his white shirt. The hard etching lines of his abodmen reveal even more runes there. Dozens of tattoos alight his skin, but at the center of his chest between his strong pectorals is the bond of Brotherhood.

"You still think you're not him?" Ruiner growls.

Malace is always so aloof and distracted. He's not in this moment. He's tragic. Haunted by a past he can't seem to remember.

"My memories are like tattered ribbons." His breath comes out shallow and uneven. "Even when they're all tied together, nothing fits right."

My hand slips out into the cold, and my fingers slide through his. His gaze is slow to travel down to where our hands are now interlocked. I want to give him more. I want to wrap my arms around him and never let this cruel kingdom touch him again.

Leavon did this to him too. Only someone powerful can create ruins. Why would Leavon destroy Malace's life just to give himself a spy?

"We'll figure this out."

"You're leaving," Malace says suddenly like an accusation. "You'll leave, and I'll remain. A man without purpose. Without care. Without life."

"Hey!" I shout as his voice fades sorrowfully.

"Don't make me take you to the human world and force you to haunt me there too."

When he looks down at me, a soft smile is shining in his crimson eyes.

"You'd do that?"

The ridiculousness of it all flutters through me, and I'm smiling right back at him. "Of course."

"You want me around that much?"

My heart skips as I hold this strange man's gaze. He's like a puppy. No matter how much chaos he creates, I'll never be able to be mad a day in my life at this beautiful man.

"I want you even more than that," I confess on barely a whisper. I take a single step toward him. My heels scuff his boots, and I still have to lean into him on the toes of my shoes. I want to kiss him. But I want him to remember it too. I don't want something like that to be tainted by Leavon's magic.

My head dips low at the last second, and I kiss the side of his sharp jaw instead.

When I pull back, his fiery eyes are shifting all across my features. There's a soft glow between us, and something inside feels so incredibly right when his hands meet the curves of my hips.

A look lingers there in the light of his eyes that he's not saying. But ever so slowly, he smiles anyway.

And for a shaking, fleeting moment I think every single thing will be okay.

WHEN I SLIDE IN THROUGH MY FAVORITE SIDE door, I travel up to the second-floor balcony at once. I didn't check in at the front door, and I find I'm the only one wearing a cloak or coat of any kind. A woman in a tight red dress curls her lip at my hood that's pulled all the way up over my shadowed features.

"Someone left the door open, and now the strays are coming in," she sneers to a woman with blue hair over her glass of wine.

I hold her gaze as I pass, her clattering diamond bracelet telling me she's not a Chosen woman but a high-ranking noble of some kind. She's only here to watch the bloodbath and place bets like the majority of the people in this room tonight.

When I step around her, a forked tail with several sharp points swooshes back and forth, catching my leg and sending me sprawling forward. My eyes are blazing when I swing back around. But she ignores me. Her laughter rakes through the room at something the other woman says. It would seem like an accident, but . . . the end of her tail lifts, and . . . did she flip me off?

My glare is still held on her while I slip out of the heavy cloak and hang it lazily over the closest chair. Her red lips fall open when my fine gown sways fully out.

"Love that dress," the blue-haired woman across from her says.

My smile is nearly a sneer when I gaze at the cruel noblewoman who tripped me. "Thank you."

"Thank you all for coming." A voice crawls over my skin like spider legs racing down my flesh. From down below, Leavon smiles out to the crowd that's circled around the long front table he's standing at. "Ten of the most beautiful, powerful women will be joining us tonight in approximately," he pauses to look up at the enormous clock face that hangs from the second-floor balcony . . . the one I'm standing right above.

His words trail off as his blazing golden eyes lock on me. My heart stops, and I spin away from his watchful stare, storming to the back of the room to hide as far away as I possibly can. I keep walking, jostling past the patrons until I come to a shining door at the very back. I shove it open, his words slipping away but lingering with me as the door softly closes.

"Twenty-five minutes," I hear him mutedly finish from inside the Great Hall.

The cold wind pulls at my dark hair. My back settles against the metal, and I take a long calming breath.

I have to make it twenty-five minutes.

I can do this.

The rain has long stopped, but the smell of it lingers in the crisp wind. It's an intoxicating scent that lifts my gaze to the night sky above the rooftop. Only to find someone else is already enjoying tonight's weather.

"Synder," I whisper. "How do you always find me?"

He sits in a golden bistro sort of chair, his pale hair blowing in the breeze. He's leaned back lazily in the seat, his arm extended to the small circular table in front of him.

It's a table for two beneath the glinting stars. A wall of metallic painted lattice is just to his right. Deep red roses climb the wooden planks. He looks like a book boyfriend come to life. It's an image of romance that most people can only dream of seeing.

A slim-cut black tuxedo hugs his body in such a way that it should be illegal to look that damn sinful. He turns fully to me, his black shirt and silk black tie blending nicely together to give him a dark allure. Everything from his shining shoes to the small cufflinks at his wrists is stark ebony . . . except for the jade-green pocket square that only shows a fraction of an inch over his heart.

It identically matches the same fine material of my dress.

"You get sick of the noblemen too?" His smile is tilted. A little tainted.

The High Fae are cruel to him. And so are the high nobles of this kingdom. It truly is a tragic realm of misfits.

"Just waiting," I say instead of the truth. The truth is: I only made it three minutes before being seen.

And I don't want to tell Synder that.

"Whatever shall we do to pass the time?"

His long fingers strum against the shining gold tabletop. The gleam in his starry eyes tells me he isn't joking. But I'm still not sure if I should make one last mistake before I leave this cursed kingdom.

Every man I've ever dated in my life has been a mistake.

Would Synder Steel be one more name on that list?

With a quiet clicking of my heels, I cross the short span of space and stop in front of this beautiful man to consider it all. Every cruel word we've said to each other circles my mind, and still, I can't say that anything we've been through has been a mistake. This dress, the stars, his smile, none of this feels like mistake.

It feels like magic.

This time, I'm in control.

"Stand up." My lips purse as I wait for him to follow my command.

His brows lift, a smile toying against his sexy-as-sin lips.

He obeys, standing ever so slowly until he's breathing down on me without touching me. Star-filled eyes shift between mine. My heart pounds. This is what it feels like to have power.

"I want to see you." My chin lifts and though I don't say it, he knows what I want.

And with a swirl of glittering magic crossing over his features, the golden boy image washes away. His hair lightens. The golden blonde color fades right out into a crisp white. His dark horns and cosmos eyes remain but the sharp angles of his face are crueler, more jagged than the perfect appearance he shows everyone else.

"A phuca," I whisper as I see him in his unfiltered light of cruelty.

The pretty boy image is like a snake's pattern: meant to lure people in. The real Synder that lies beneath his veil of magic, it's fitting. It's a hard and jaded look that I feel like I've known even before he revealed it.

"I can be whoever I want to be."

"Except you don't choose to be you." My words sting my heart and it only hurts more when he looks away from that honesty.

He . . . hates himself. It's clearer now that the smooth arrogance isn't there to shield his features.

With a single step, I close the distance between us.

My palm presses over his heart, the sleek pocket square skimming beneath my fingertips. At the last second, I pull the pocket square from his suit. A questioning smirk alights his face as I tuck it down my cleavage and into my dress for safe keeping.

A memento. A single perfect moment that I actually want to remember from this tainted city.

"You're beautiful," I whisper and it only makes him smirk even more with disbelief.

With my hand against his chest, I lightly push him away from his golden seat. One step after the other, he gives me space. A dry breath hits my throat as I realize just how real this is. And then I quickly take action.

My heel teeters on the chair, but I only linger there for a moment before hopping up to sit on the brick ledge of the balcony. The full moon hangs above, hundreds of Carnals walk below. And then there's us, suspended in this beautiful moment of possibilities.

"What do you want, Bellatrix?" he asks on a tone of pure gravel, his tongue sliding out to roll across his lower lip.

Everything blooms to life in my chest as little by little, I pull at the edge of my pretty gown. It bunches in my hands. Soon there's fistfuls of the wrinkled fabric in my hands. The cold breeze licks across my thighs until there's nothing at all separating me from him.

"Come here," I whisper on a surprisingly even, sultry voice.

He prowls toward me, his galaxy eyes darkening the closer he gets. His chest brushes against the lacy material covering my breasts. He's so near, I want to lean into him even more and close the distance.

"Well?" he asks darkly.

"Get on your knees."

Silver flashes through the wells of his hooded eyes.

Big hands skim over my knees, racing shivers up my thighs. And then he lowers.

The breath in my lungs catches. He never once lowers his gaze. I can't look away. When he's on the ground, bowing before me, I say what I've been thinking for too long.

"Fuck me with that cruel, cruel mouth of yours, Synder."

The twitch of his lips is barely seen before his head dips down, the light warmth of his breath fanning over me, making me shift with anticipation. Soft lips skim my thigh. Then intense heat lashes across my pussy. He laps me up slowly, tasting me like he never wants to forget. When his tongue swirls higher, he focuses there, sucking hard before relenting to press over my clit all over again with another hard flick. The wind catches my moans as my head tilts back. Over and over and over again, he repeats that tormenting process until my fluttering lashes open, and I'm crying out to the starry heavens above. Lightning flashes across the darkness while waves and waves of reckless tingles crash through my body. My fingers fist through soft hair before hitting the hard exterior of spiraling horns. I hold on there. With both hands, I use him as leverage, grinding my sex against him until my hips are fucking his sinful mouth to the very brink of ecstasy.

Big hands jerk my hips forward, pressing him even harder against my clit until blinding light flashes behind my eyes. My moans are a melody that matches the thunder above as my orgasm shatters all through me on wrecking waves.

I haven't even caught my breath before he's lifting me and dragging me forward. He falls into the golden chair and brings me right down on top of the apparent hardness that's pressing against his thin layer of clothing. Casually, he rocks his rigid length against me, pulling a breath from my lungs at the mere pressure he's putting against my swollen sex.

I'm still holding his horns. He's smiling up at me like I'm the most sinful creature he has ever laid eyes on. His hand slips between us, cold fingers slide across my wetness, and his smile grows. His other hand holds on against the curve of my ass as he leans in close, his lips ghosting along mine.

"No one's ever going to fuck you like I do, baby," he promises once more.

The night I spent with Ruin and Malace flashes behind my eyes, and the shame I thought I'd feel for thinking of them . . . it isn't there.

Synder isn't a possessive man. The way he phrases that promise alone tells me he doesn't think he owns me.

"And what if someone else does?" I challenge.

His fingers roll across my clit, tearing a gasp from my lungs and pulling a wicked smirk to his lips.

"Then I guess I'll have to try harder," he whispers across my lips before pressing a slow, demanding kiss there.

My hips react to every teasing movement of his hand. Between kisses, I ask the most confusing question.

"Does the idea of me being with someone else not make you crazy?"

His head shakes, but he doesn't stop the slow press of his lips to mine.

"I've never owned anything in my entire life. I can't start with something as salient as you."

Two fingers shove deeply into me, and my moan is devoured, his kiss pressing hard as he fucks me with his hand even harder.

My palms are sliding down the fine press of his tuxedo, making haste to get to the black belt that's hidden beneath his jacket. The buckle falls open, but a sharp edge slices along my finger as I pull away.

It's a minor cry of pain, but he hears it. And he stops abruptly. He pulls back from me. His hand lifts to mine, and he cradles my palm in his. A drop of blood slides down my index finger, and he watches it intently. So intently, I lift my hand and bring it to his lips. They part but not nearly enough. The crimson color slides over his lips, and the pink of his tongue slips out to take me into the warmth of his mouth. His eyes close with a look of pure pleasure.

And it's then that I push down his pants, and ever so slowly, slide my sex along the hard length of his cock. A groan rumbles across my finger, and he releases my hand to grip my curves tightly.

"Fuck me. Please," he begs, and I love the sound of it. His dark voice is laced with a growling, threatening tone, but the words he speaks are pleading.

He's letting me own him. Or at least, he's trying to. He just isn't used to relenting to someone, I don't think. That alone makes me want him even more.

The tip of his pulsing cock grinds across my clit, and I take my time watching the alighted neediness brighten his dark eyes.

"Please," he whispers more gently against my lips. His words are softer, but his hands on my hips are painful. They're the hands of a man who isn't used to asking for anything.

It's his kiss that makes me weak though. All the pretty words in the world are nothing compared to the slow, dominating way he kisses me.

My hands wrap around his smooth horns once more as I lift myself. As much as he tries to give me power, his hands are greedy. He shoves my hips down hard, but I fight him for it. I buck against his strength. Inch by inch, it's a push and pull of our bodies as I enjoy the slickness of his cock working me ever so slowly. It's a war between us. A fight to see who will finish first.

If I even let him finish at all.

At the last second, I give in. And his palms slam my hips down until his length is as deep as he can possibly go.

"Fucckk," he hisses against my jagged gasp.

The galaxy in his eyes shines up to me as I thrust down him on a slow, torturing rhythm. Deeper he tries to grind into me, but I don't let him. I hold his horns and set the pace that's making me wetter and wetter with every hard inch he sinks into me.

When I slide down slowly the next time . . . it's almost painful. My eyes widen. His smile tilts mischievously.

"That's the thing about Phucas and Shapeshifters, things can be as big—or as thick—as I need them to be." He pauses, remembering who's in charge. "As *you* want them to be."

I nod, and that's the only signal he needs. My walls stretch as he takes control, fucking me at a faster pace that spirals trembling energy all through my core. He stretches me even more, pulsing his thickness in such an extreme way it makes me insane with lust. He fucks me even harder. I'm barely hanging on as his pace becomes violent and unforgiving.

The cry of my moans carries through the cold, cruel wind. It twirls my hair around us. Thunder cracks, shaking through my chest and into his.

And then rain pours down across our entangled bodies. Raindrops thrum against my flesh, and I find myself meeting his punishing thrusts, wanting more, needing to find the edge that's so damn close now.

He's slick against me. He's demanding. He wants my stubborn release more than I do.

And then he gives it to me.

He slams in hard, thrusting as deep as he can go and then even more. My head tips back to the rain as my entire body shakes in his arms. Then it all washes over me. Splattering colors flicker as my eyes tightly close, and everything unravels.

He keeps going, dragging out the wild sensation for several minutes before he, too, is groaning along my neck.

We're as close as we possibly can be, and I just want to stay like that forever. He holds me, uncaring of the storm raining down on us and drenching our fine clothes.

He never does let me go.

Until the chiming of an ominous clock rings out. A fearful scream follows that sound. And then my heart drops.

The festivities have begun.

CHAPTER TWENTY

WHEN THE DOOR closes quietly behind us, screams of agony fill the room. But the patrons on the second level are all seated calmly, their heads angled to see over the railing at the events below. Magic glints across Synder's face, morphing him into that golden boy appearance once more. My heart stutters to see him hide himself away again. He follows behind me at a slow pace, putting distance between the two of us as we quickly rush to the edge of the balcony.

Just near the stairs, I peer down at the spanning floor below.

Ten women of all ages are scrambling across the open space. A redhead leaps atop a table and comes crashing down with a chair in tow. Her strength seems magnified. It's nothing like I've ever seen before. It breaks over the head of an older woman. The wood severs right through the woman's skull, and she falls face-first to the tile floor. Her body lands so harshly, the stone cracks beneath the weight of the blow of the redhead. And then she's striding out to find her next victim.

Anxiety rips painfully through me. I'm searching the chaotic space. Blood and debris are everywhere, but I can't find Ivy.

Leavon stands at the foot of the stairs, just near the side door hallway, and though I can barely see him, Malace stands there, too, his face pale and disgusted as he steps aside for two women beating each other with violent hooves and talons.

Leavon touches Malace's shoulder. Even from here, I can see the way his body stiffens at Leavon's touch. Something is whispered between them. Malace's jaw ticks, and instead of replying, he walks away with his hands in his pockets like the anarchy around him is just another beautiful walk in the park.

He gets lost in the violence that's thrashing through the room, but the glare Leavon pins to my friend's back is clear as day. Leavon hates him. Despises him even.

I have to find Ivy.

Before it's too late.

Before she ends up hurt, or worse, she ends up hurting someone she cares about. Just like I did.

My heels are silenced as I glide quietly down the dark stairwell. At the bottom, my shoes slide over the flooring, nearly taking me down fast.

I lift my heavy, wet dress and find particles dusting

the tile. They're hard to see, but the grit of it grinds under my shoe.

"Sand," I whisper.

He's right on the other side of this wall. The held breath in my lungs is painful. I peer out just slightly. Golden hair is combed to perfection, and his back is fully to me. He's distracted.

It's then that I dart out.

The moment I'm on the main floor, I'm fair game, it seems.

I spot blonde curls, and my heart leaps as I chase after the girl in the cornflower blue gown. I'm not the only one though. Another woman a bit older than myself stalks behind Ivy. Sharp, elongated fingers lift, and she rips them high in the air to bring them down with brutal force. With a quick rush, I snatch her and pull her elbow back, twisting her creepy arm away from my oblivious sister. Ivy sneaks on through the crowd without incident.

"Look at me," I command.

Her glare meets mine, but the fury in it disappears the moment my trance catches her.

"You're going to cross this room. You'll see a closet door in the far corner. Go inside. And lock it. Do not come out until it's quiet. Do you understand?" I ask as peacefully as I can for someone who's holding this woman hostage at the moment.

Her blank-stare shines up at me. She says nothing.

I wait, but . . . I don't have fucking time for this

I release her and watch for a second as she staggers toward the corner of the room.

"Thank fuck," I whisper at the one good thing I've done right since I got to this cursed Kingdom.

I turn on my heels to find Ivy once more. A little girl is standing right in front of me, though, no older than ten or so. Her pretty, curled pigtails sway as she turns to look innocently up at me. And then she rushes me. Her petite shoulder hits my stomach, and she takes me down like a fucking linebacker. My hands grip her little wrists to try to stop the child from hurting herself, but when I look up at her features, snarling, jagged teeth are snapping out at my face. I shove her twisted features away, but her rows of teeth nick my thumb.

I'm conflicted about hurting a small child, but at the moment, all I want to do is punt this little demon girl across the room.

She's jerked off of me and thrown to the side before I have to make that choice. My lashes lift, and a familiar smile is shining down on me.

"Who knew Gremlins could be so vicious," Ivy says as she nods at the wicked little devil girl.

"Gremlins. Great."

"I don't think you're allowed to help me." She side-steps two women who are literally pulling each other's hair out and for what?

Leavon? A man with a fucking unkempt skin condition? Are his promises really worth all the bloodshed?

"Ivy, you shouldn't do this. Leavon can't strengthen

your power. You can do that. I can help. He offers nothing and takes everything."

She's barely listening though as a new woman with fangs lunges at her.

"Iv—" My words are cut short when I have to tear the bitch off of my little sister.

But Ivy doesn't relent. There's a manic glint in her eyes that only the darkest of magic can ignite. She isn't herself right now. She's enhanced with a Monster inside of her, and that Monster is feeding off of this chaos.

With the splintered remains of a destroyed chair, Ivy grips a broken wooden chair leg and slams it through the woman's chest. The woman's empty scream is cut short. Blood gushes down Ivy's hand, and she lowers the woman to the floor with ease.

It's done.

She has killed someone. And I don't know how to look away from the blood on her hands. I know when she realizes what she has done, neither will she.

"Ivy," I say on a shaking breath. "Ivy." She's walking away. "Ivy, I'm your sister!" I scream to her.

Her steps halt immediately. Behind her, Ruiner stands near the doors, his hard gaze set on me.

"Let me take you home. We need to leave. This place is toxic. Leavon is toxic. And if you stay . . ."

I can't say it.

I can't say it because I'm terrified Synder is right. No Chosen woman has ever survived. Except me.

And if it comes down to Ivy or me, it's a simple choice. It'll always be her. I'd let her kill me.

"You're not my sister. I don't have a sister," Ivy finally replies coldly, but I can hear the uncertainty in her tone.

"I am. My name's Bellatrix Cuore. I was born with a heart condition, and when you were born, you were the healthiest, strongest little girl I'd ever met. You were my opposite. My other half." Her eyes narrow on me, so I keep going. "Every Sunday, Dad would make chocolate chip pancakes, and Mom would make us go to church. We *loved* the pancakes. The church . . ." I shrug in an indifferent way that only a sister can show.

"How do you know that about my parents?"

My lips part, but she cuts me off.

"You're a liar. You lied about that girl who was my roommate, and you're lying now!"

The fighting of the room never stops for us, but it does the moment his patient footfalls carry across the bloody floor.

"Ladies, ladies. This is not how I conduct my festivities." Leavon's bronze suit blends in to his golden skin, and when his shining eyes slide to me, bile burns at the back of my throat.

"Remove the rune on her," I order.

Ivy glances from me to Leavon and then back again.

His smile is a cutting thing when he looks me dead in the eyes. "Trix, you and I both know if I remove the repression rune, it won't change her mind. She'll want to stay. Just like all the others."

The use of that name, the name that only he used for me, slams into me like a knife. He remembers. Maybe he knew I'd come all along.

That's why he chose Ivy.

To get to me.

"Then remove it." My head lifts, and I have total confidence in my sister. I have more confidence in her than I've ever faked for myself in my entire life. "Remove it!" I demand through clenched teeth.

"Say you'll stay. Say you'll consider my offer, Trix, and I'll clear her mind of the repression and the darkness that's clouding her thoughts."

Ruiner walks the floor then, striding closer to me at the sound of that trade. My jaw grinds, but I remember what my friend said. Only great magic like Leavon's can fix what Ivy has been through.

And so I nod.

"I will."

"A smart choice." Leavon smiles and lifts his hand. Sand sifts through his fingertips as he gently pushes back my sister's blonde locks. His thumb brushes down her bottom lip, and I could pull the steak out of Vampira's chest right now to murder this motherfucker for touching her. But then he speaks. "Eradicate repress. Illuminate logic," he whispers strangely.

A jolt strikes through her. Her small shoulder shake. She blinks.

And then she looks around the room. Until her attention lands on me.

My heartbeat strums, picking up a tune until it's a frantic song that's drilling through my chest.

"Bella?" she finally whispers on a sob. Her hands lift, trembling so hard I want to hold her. "Bella, please take me home. Please. Please. Come with me. Don't stay here. You can't stay here." Her words all meld together, but I feel him watching us.

My dress billows as I kneel down at her side. I hold her head in my hands. Tears stream down her face, making her look younger than her thirteen years.

"I'll take you home," I whisper to her. "Everything's going to be alright. We're going home. I promise."

When I look up, Leavon's arrogant smile turns twisting.

He truly did take her and torment her and let all of these girls die.

Just to get to me.

Sand twirls violently then. It sprays across my face, and I have to shield my eyes to peer up at the man who looks more like a cruel god than a Monster.

"You lie! You'll never bow to me! You never have! Unless I have something you want." With rushing sand, he strikes out. His magic drags at my sister's hair. She's ripped away from me with violent strength. The blue gown tears on a table leg as she's pulled across the floor, and I run after her, fear blooming through my heart with every step I take.

My hands grapple at the ends of her dress, but he's too fast. The doors fling open with unseen magic. They're gone in seconds.

She's gone.

With the slamming of my heart, I never stop following the sound of her screams. Chairs and tables fly through the room among a sandstorm of vehemence. Something slams painfully into my leg, but I keep going.

"Bella!" someone calls gruffly from behind me, but I'm already running out into the dark night. Rain lashes down from the heavens as sand scratches at my flesh. I rush into the thick of it. It swirls faster and faster. The growing power of it is the only reason I know at all that I'm going the right way.

Soon gleaming light swirls out, and I know where I am when the platform comes into view. Falhorns beat their hooves on hard steel as the carousel turns slow at first. And then quickly turns reckless and rapid. It lifts slightly off the wet grass, and fear strikes through my heart at what I know the dark creatures are used for.

They travel through kingdoms at a speed only they're capable of.

If Leavon leaves, I'll never see her again. I won't know where they've gone or what he's done with her for the rest of my life.

"Bella," her little voice cries out, and with a strong leap, I catch the nearest bar. The jerk of it shakes through my body, pulling painfully at my arm. A horned horse stomps ahead of me as my sister kicks and screams. Leavon throws her onto the saddle, his sand pulling away along his skull before fully forming his features.

"Little useless bitch," he seethes.

Synder unties the Falhorn from its station, and when his head lifts, his pretty eyes are tragic as he holds my gaze.

"Hurry up!" Leavon growls at him.

And it's enough to tear away Synder's attention. He throws his leg over the jet-black Falhorn opposite of Leavon. He peers back at me one last time. A lifetime of regret shines in his starry eyes.

I lunge for them.

But with a loud boom, the demon horses storm forward, billowing black smoke all around them.

And then they're gone.

The platform pulls at my frame, but I stagger with every step. My knees hit the floor hard, but I pull myself up to the other Falhorn tied at the horns. I fumble with the reigns, but I pull the tie away. I drag myself up its enormous frame. My fingers hold tight to the black leather of its bindings. I hunch forward.

I'm fucking ready.

"Bella! Bella, what the fuck are you doing?" Ruin catches my arm. Malace stands at his side, but the ghost is much quicker to react.

He grabs ahold of the creature's saddle and pulls himself up behind me.

"Are you two out of your fucking minds? Get down! Please. Bella, please! Listen to me!" I only look at him for a moment as the beast stomps its heavy hooves. His bright blue eyes aren't filled with fury for once. They're filled with fear.

"I'm sorry," I yell as my hair blows across my face in the vicious wind.

Ruin shakes his head helplessly before leaping onto the Falhorn behind me. The entire world shakes around us. Ruin's stream of pleading words is still heard over the thunderous magic of the beasts.

But I made up my mind a long time ago. I'm not leaving Ivy to this monstrous world.

I'll never leave her with Leavon.

The gears of the mechanics break away, clattering to the floor with lashing sparks. The wind and sand turn violent. A zap of lightening crackles through the platform, rattling the floor beneath impatient hooves. Smoke rises up all around me. My breath catches in my chest as we're lunged forward. Everything goes dark.

And then we disappear.

The End.

More chaotic monsters are coming in book two, *Of Monsters and Mania* NEXT MONTH!!!

Get your copy here:

Of Monsters and Mania

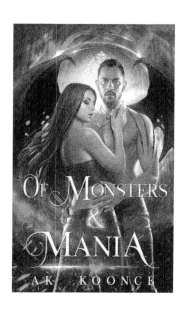

Monsters devour fear, cruelty, and torment.
Apparently, *the Fae do too.*

Get your copy here:

Of Monsters and Mania

Or turn the page for an exclusive (unedited) sneak peek at *Of Monsters and Mania*!

OF MONSTERS AND MANIA
PROLOGUE

THREE DECADES Earlier

The most beautiful fae baby was born on the first snow-fallen night of the winter solstice. His eyes were bright as the ice that covered the lamp lights. His father was a Nobleman on the upper side of the Kingdom of Aurulent. The High Fae King had congratulated him personally on the birth of his first son.

It was decided he would take his father's name: Rune. A name of powerful magic and respect.

Until...

"His wings, they're not pure," the old midwife maiden whispered, halting her swaddling and looking abruptly to the mother instead of the looming father. Disgust ran lines across the Nobleman's face. His glare raced from the small baby boy to the fearful eyes of the mother lying in the birthing bed.

"No!" the mother screamed.

But it was too late.

The white cloth was ripped away and the child laid naked. Stark leathery wings protruded from his shoulder blades where soft pure wings should have grown. What was seen when the nobleman harshly turned the infant over was much, much worse.

"Monster!" The man hissed in the room full of emotionally worn women. "Get rid of it!" the father —*man*—seethed.

He swung from the cold, dark room before the sobs of his young wife could fully exhale. His storming boots were heard down the long corridor even over the howls of the midnight winds.

The maiden flinched through the cries of the mother who begged her to save her baby. Her agony wouldn't live on in the maiden's mind though. This moment of torment was one of many. Monsters were not to be kept. It was fae law. And Mauddalin was very used to these tragedies in her forty-one years of being a midwife maiden.

Two other women held the hysterical mother down as Mauddalin discreetly grabbed a thicker, warmer blanket. She quickly wrapped the monster in the cloth as she'd done a thousand times. Without even getting to see its mother, the creature was carried from the bedchamber, down the long corridor, and right out to the night cold.

A garbage bin sat at the edge of the regal cottage and once she was side by side with it, the maiden looked up at the dark windows of the estate. Empty glass was all that looked down on her. No one was watching.

Then she passed the bin and rushed out into the snow. Her boots sunk deeper and deeper as she journeyed into the frost-bitten evening. Mauddalin had done this job for forty-one years. And there was a profit in it for fae babies born of impure lineage.

A man by the name of Leavon Sandstorme had taught her that.

Her knuckles rapt across the mysterious man's door. The unforgiving wind stung across her cheeks and the wails of the newborn were far louder than any knock ever could be.

The worn door opened with a slivering crack.

"Hello?" the man called out, not revealing his face but hiding behind the safety of his home.

"I—I have another one," Mauddalin stuttered. "It's from Lord Rune's manor."

She didn't know what the strange man used all the monstrous babies for. She only knew his pay was enough to cover her bills and keep food on the table for her own children over the last several years.

"Another good child," the man reminisced with a crackling chuckle that made her skin crawl.

From between the splintered framing of the door, a hand wandered out. The flesh of it was bone dry, flaking away in the harsh wind like sand in a time turner.

Coins dropped to the snow without a sound before that hand retreated back into the depths of the dark home.

"Leave it on the steps," he commanded with a rattling slam of the door.

And as she'd done a thousand times before, Mauddalin covered the child's pink face with the warmth of the blanket, scooped up her earnings, and rushed off into the shadow ridden night.

As for the monster, he'd be used to the full extent of his purchase price.

And someday, he'd win Leavon Sandstorme a Kingdom of his own.

Get your copy here:

Of Monsters and Mania

ALSO BY A.K. KOONCE

Reverse Harem Books

The To Tame a Shifter Series

Taming

Claiming

Maiming

Sustaining

Reigning

The Monsters and Miseries Series

Hellish Fae

Sinless Demons

Spiteful Creatures

The Rejected Realms Series

Hell Kissed

Fire Kissed

Soul Kissed

The Villainous Wonderland Series

Into the Madness

The Lost Fae

The Midnight Monsters Series

ABOUT THE AUTHOR

A.K. Koonce is a USA Today bestselling author. She's a mom by day and a fantasy and paranormal romance writer by night. She keeps her fantastical stories in her mind on an endless loop while she tries her best to focus on her actual life and not that of the spectacular, but demanding, fictional characters who always fill her thoughts.

If you want more A.K. Koonce updates, deleted scenes, and giveaways, join her Newsletter or Facebook Reader Group!
AK Koonce Newsletter
AK Koonce Reading Between Realms Facebook Group

Printed in Great Britain
by Amazon